Not Enough Midnights

Book Two: Six Guns and Sorcery

MICHAEL MERRIAM

DREY BOOKS
P.O. Box 5652
Hopkins, MN 55343

Drey Books
P.O. Box 5256
Hopkins, MN 55343

Printed in the United States of America

ACKNOWLEDGEMENTS

The author would like to gratefully acknowledge:
- The Oklahoma Historical Society for their large collection of early statehood photographs;
- Tim Uren, whose stage production of H. P. Lovecraft's "The Curse of Yig" started the seed of this piece;
- Marty Robbins, whose album "Gunfighter Ballads and Trail Songs" played on constant repeat during the writing.

Special thanks to Kate Bitters for the wonderful cover art and Eli Effinger-Weintraub for being the best editor ever.

DEDICATION

This one is for the people of Caddo County, Oklahoma.

ONE

"The window shutters! Stuff them in the window shutters!"

Thomas McHenry followed his wife's directions, cramming one of his spare shirts in the small cracks as Mary finished pushing towels under the one door into their home. Thomas cast a quick look at Jeb. The blue-tick hound was backed in to a corner, whimpering.

I need wood, Thomas thought. Flat planks of solid building wood would help seal the windows and doors tight, but all the wood he owned was stored in the barn. He would be dead and damned if he dared the barn.

Thomas was no coward. A coward would never have survived homesteading in the wild Oklahoma Territory for the last nine months. He and Mary left Georgia in search of good soil to plant seeds and a place to put down family roots. The modest patch of land outside of Hennessey Corner seemed a dream come true. Thomas built the snug wood frame house last summer, replacing the original dugout. Mary put in a vegetable garden, and the dark red soil was good for cotton, just like back home. Chickens, a mule, a horse, a milk cow, and a few hogs for the slaughter made the McHenry homestead perfect. He glanced over at Mary, the fabric of her plain brown dress near her belly showing the soft swell of the child she carried in her womb, their second.

Her eyes were wide as she took two steps back from the door. "Oh God. The Fosters. This must be what happened to Richard and Ellen." The hissing from outside home nearly drowned out her voice, filled the space despite how tight they had closed the doors and windows.

They had ignored the drums. At least, they had ignored them as much as possible. Granny Creswell from Hennessey Corner had warned them the local Caddo and Wichita tribes set up the racket with their drums all through the fall harvest. Day and night the drums beat out their constant rhythm, though no one knew why the annual event happened and no one could find the drummers themselves. The drumming seemed to come from every corner of the land, echoing down the buttes and into the small canyons, across the creeks and over the fields day and night without stopping, until they faltered two months ago, ending as suddenly as they started. The silence seemed a blessing.

Oh, how wrong they had all been.

The Fosters were the first to vanish. Like the McHenrys, they were new to Hennessey Corner, their little place close to the rising butte the locals called Crying Woman Mound, where the drums always seemed loudest.

Richard Foster missed the last town meeting, where he and Thomas were part of a group agitating to coax the new Enid and Anadarko Railroad to build a branch line into Hennessey Corner. They wanted the train to stop at the local cotton gins, replacing the slow and expensive draft wagons that took the bales of cotton to either Binger or the settlement around Fort Cobb for shipment to market. They had argued that the train stop would bring more business and progress to the sleepy crossroads town.

Thomas had gone looking for his friend, only to find the Fosters' livestock—any that hadn't run off—wandering aimlessly about the property and no sign of the family, though all their possessions were in the dugout. It looked as if they'd simply up and walked away from the farm, except he found no tracks indicating the family of five had indeed walked off. None of the Fosters were heard from again. Marshal Rich, the lawman in Hennessey Corner, declined to pursue the mystery since it was outside the town borders. The county sheriff suggested hiring a private investigator. The U.S. Marshal's office was busy chasing the Dalton gang.

Mary's scream brought him back to the present. The door, nailed shut and boarded up with the few pieces of wood in the house, rattled under a blow from the outside

The weird hissing rose like the winds of a prairie thunderstorm. Jeb whimpered and howled, setting off the McHenrys' four-year-old daughter Laura, who screamed and burst into tears. Mary picked up Laura, clutching her close. Thomas lifted the axe; his rifle as out in the yard, empty and useless.

The front door tattled again, bowed a bit in the center, straining the lead nails holding the single wooden plank in place as dust drifted down from the rafters. It was enough of a crack to allow the first few snakes to slip inside the McHenry home. Thomas charged, swinging down with his axe, screaming at the rattling creatures crawling toward his family. He caught a glimpse of Mary climbing up in the bed, still holding Laura close as she pointed his revolver at the floor. The door shuddered again as he cut two snakes in half. Jeb finally joined the fray, his survival instincts overriding the terror threating to debilitate them all.

He hacked at another snake as a third terrible thump shook the door, cracking the frame and allowing a seemingly never-ending slither of serpents to pour into the house. Jeb whined, snapping at the rattler attached his hindquarter. Thomas wheeled to the slice the snake attacking his hound, axe raised. Behind him, the window shutter crashed and splintered.

Mary screamed, high and wild. Thomas turned, his axe at the ready before dropping it to the floor, the nerves in his fingers suddenly gone cold as Mary and Laura vanished out the broken hole where there had been a window and into the dark, gripped by two enormous scaly hands. He heard the gun fire twice and a small piece of his mind that clung to sanity prayed to God that Mary had killed Laura and then taken her own life.

Thomas looked down at the snakes pooled around his boots, slithering up his legs and clinging to his thighs, teeth in his flesh, puncturing through the rough pants he wore. He swayed and looked up at the shattered hole in the wall his wife and children had vanished through.

The fangs, gleaming white and long as his skinning knives, filled his vision before the massive maw closed over his head and around his neck.

Thomas twitched once before the blessing of death took him.

TWO

I stepped down onto the wooden platform as the parked train huffed and smoked at my back. Adjusting the small pack I carried on my left shoulder, I gave the town of Binger, Oklahoma Territory, a quick inspection, my eyes sweeping the long red-dirt main street. It was...unremarkable: a bank, hotel, and territorial post office; four saloons, a pair of newspapers, the jail, stables, a grocer, and a department store. Small wood-framed houses on the side streets made up the rest of the town. I could see a cotton gin at one end of the street, its loading doors next to the railroad spur. A small stockyard was built further on up the street, thankfully downwind today. There was no passenger depot, just the raised platform I stood on and a little canvas-covered overhang to keep freight and mail out of the worst of the any rain. The most interesting thing was the young man standing on an upside-down shipping crate and crying out like a firebrand preacher that the end was coming and the true gods of the land would walk among them again. I frowned at the man's crazy speech. Still, except for the lone madman, Binger could have been any of the hundred prairie towns I had seen over the decades.

It could have been Cold Springs, before the monster.

I shook my head to clear the dark thoughts. It was the people that caught my attention. I'd spent most of my adult life being a lawman and could spot the fear running through the townsfolk in their brisk walk from building to building and in the wariness of their eyes as they studied the passengers leaving the train while trying to watch every direction at once. I could see it in the tight nods and frowning faces. Even the local dogs were hushed and quiet, as if terrified to draw attention.

Whatever danger the locals feared would be the reason a

telegram from the office of President Benjamin Harrison himself had arrived at my police precinct house in San Francisco, requesting me to travel to Binger, Oklahoma Territory, there to be briefed by the local deputy marshal in a situation that required "special knowledge of creatures and matters most unnatural." If my time in the army and as a marshal had taught me anything, it was that a request from the office of the president wasn't really a request. The San Francisco Police had detached me to the U.S. Marshals, and my Millie had sternly admonished me to not get my fool-self killed or eaten as she packed my bags and handed me a train ticket to the Oklahoma territorial capital of Guthrie, there to switch to a train to Fort Reno and then on to Binger.

I smiled at the two familiar people walking down the platform toward me, my gloomy mood lifting as I held out my hand to William Blenchy, former Deputy United States Marshal. "Bill, it's good to see you again."

"Married life looks like it agrees with you, Jefferson." Blenchy was as tall and thin as I remembered and his mustache as large as ever, if a little grayer. He wore a nice charcoal suit instead of his former buckskins and boots, no doubt the influence of his own woman. His Colt rested in its worn leather holster, held up by a plain black gun belt, and the gray wide-brimmed hat on his head looked almost new.

"Three meals and a warm bed do wonders for a man."

Blenchy grunted his agreement as I turned to the second member of my greeting party, taking off my hat and giving her a nod. "Lady Priscilla, I see you're still riding herd over this ne'er-do-well," I said, glancing toward Blenchy. "When is Bill going to make you an honest woman?"

Lady Priscilla Talbot was tall for a woman, though Bill Blenchy still towered over her. She wore a brown riding skirt and matching vest over a white blouse. Her chestnut hair was swept up under a small hat. She carried a parasol in her gloved hands.

They had both been there with me that terrible night in Cold Springs, Nebraska. Lady Priscilla's father had died there, his heart failing as we battled the demon that had decimated the town. I knew they had been through the fire and out the other side. There were few people I trusted as I did William Blenchy and Lady Priscilla Talbot.

"Please, Jefferson, just Priscilla," she said with a light laugh, her English accent out of place in this dusty little frontier town. "And I've always been an honest woman, if not an innocent one."

"I keep asking her," Blenchy said. He frowned at Priscilla, but his love for her never faded from his eyes. "She thinks we shouldn't because of…her condition."

I didn't know enough about Lady Priscilla's being a werewolf to understand what the risks might be to her husband or any child she would carry and bear. Did she fear Blenchy would have to kill her if she lost control of the wolf within her? Could she pass her condition to her child? No, I didn't understand at all, and I refused to put forth any opinion on the matter. This was a decision between husband and wife, which they truly were even if Priscilla refused his proposals until death claimed one of them. I nodded and held my tongue on the matter. "Any of you heard from Bloom?" I asked into the following silence. Mr. Arkady Bloom was the fourth survivor of Cold Springs, though he had been gravely wounded.

"He sends his regards," Lady Priscilla said.
Blenchy nodded. "We saw him last winter for a bit."
"Oh?"

"I had to return to England to complete and close several of father's business dealings," Lady Priscilla said. "There were creditors to pay, patents to file, buildings and equipment to sell. It was all quite boring and tedious."

I reached down for the one Gladstone I'd brought along from San Francisco, but Blenchy beat me to it, lifting the bag my wife had surely over-packed as easily as he would a small child. We stepped off the wooden platform, and I followed Blenchy and Lady Priscilla toward the hotel, where I hoped the answers to all my questions waited. And maybe a meal to go with those answers, as well.

The Binger Hotel was a two-story building, twice as deep and wide as the houses on the side streets. The hotel boasted long porches with wood rails on both floors facing the street and a sign hanging from the corner post that simply said "Rooms." The hotel's name was painted across the side of the building in red. The lobby was polished dark woods with a brass and glass chandelier hanging in the center. The man behind the counter passed me a key and signaled for a boy of about thirteen to carry my bag to the second-floor room after I signed the book. I tossed the boy a couple of pennies and adjusted my gun belt. Feeling a little nostalgic, I'd brought along my old cavalry Schofield and I'd forgotten how the weight of the heavier pistol settled on the belt. I turned to find Blenchy, who had followed.

"Priscilla's waiting in the lobby with Marshal Thomas. We're staying next door to you." Blenchy paused. "We've got this three-room thing, since she brought her maid along." He paused again, chewing his bottom lip. "Violet is, well, she's different for sure."

I felt my eyebrows rise at Blenchy's tone. "Well then, I look forward to meeting her. In the meantime, let's go see your woman and this Marshal Thomas."

U.S. Deputy Marshal Henry "Heck" Thomas was of medium height and had a mustache to rival Blenchy's on a round face. He wore his pistol in the classic cavalryman's cross draw style. His badge—the same badge I had worn for years—was pinned to his coat. He stood and held out a hand. "Captain Jefferson Stottlemyre, it is a pleasure to meet you, sir."

I wanted to chuckle at the title. This was the third time I'd been a captain: in the Federal army during the war, as Deputy U.S. Marshal in Dakota Territory, and now with the San Francisco police.

"The same, Marshal Thomas," I said. My respect for him was genuine. He was one of the men charged with keeping the peace and enforcing the law in the ever-dangerous

Oklahoma and Indian Territories. From reading the newsprint stories, I knew he was the lead marshal chasing the Dalton gang. I glanced over at the older man, maybe in his early sixties, sitting in a high back chair near Marshal Thomas. He wore a badge as well. The town marshal, I realized. He wore gray trousers, a white shirt and black string tie and vest. His hat sat in his lap. I nodded in acknowledgement.

"This is Dan Widner," Thomas said. "He's a friend."

Widner held out a hand. "Captain Stottlemyre."

I shook the man's hand, settled into my chair across from them, and took a sip from the glass of water placed on a side table by the same boy who carried up my bag. I glanced at Blenchy and Lady Priscilla, but they seemed to be waiting from me to take the lead. Fair enough. I leaned forward in my chair and looked Marshal Thomas straight in the eyes. "Now, why don't you tell me why President Harrison felt the need to drag my old bones out from California? Because the last time I got a letter from Washington, it was to inform me that my commission as revoked."

I was surprised that Jefferson had made the trip from California. Thankful, but surprised. The way the government treated him after the Cold Springs disaster should have left him bitter, but Jefferson had just shrugged as if he'd expect the government to lay all the responsibility at his feet and gone on with his life.

It was no one's fault the train had been forced to stop in Cold Springs, Nebraska, and we had fought the monster we found there with everything we had while trying to survive the attacks of what had seemed an indestructible foe. Jefferson had kept his head, kept us working together. And while it was ultimately Priscilla who had killed the creature with a combination of dynamite and poor dead Wulf's fancy energy pistol, it was Jefferson who had led us through and out of our desperate battle.

15

There had been casualties, too many casualties. The entire train crew, the special railroad agent, the inventors—including Priscilla's father—others civilians Jefferson and I had been charged to protect had fallen under the creature's onslaught. Someone had to take the blame for the disaster, and the folks back in Washington decided that someone would be Jefferson.

I resigned my own commission as a deputy marshal, my anger at the situation and my desire to pursue the hand of Lady Priscilla Talbot, who for some reason was as taken with me as I with her, pushing me to change my life. You should be careful with your wishes. Oh, don't get me wrong; I'm pleased at how my life has turned. I got all the change I could want and more. Over the last two years, while working on behalf of her beloved British government, Priscilla and I had chased and dealt with creatures that would have driven strong men to nightmares. Our latest mission had taken us to British Columbia to put down a Wendigo. Two members of the North-West Mounted Police and our Blackfoot tracker died on the claws of the flesh-eater, good men all lost before we took the monster down for good and ever.

The telegraph waiting at Fort Hamilton had surprised me. My first thought was to refuse, but Priscilla, always sensible, talked me into returning to the States for the first time since Cold Springs. My one requirement was for Jefferson Stottlemyre to be part of the mission, if he agreed. I was surprised at how quickly the folks in Washington approved my demand. Deputy Marshal Thomas's explanation helped me understand why they had been so quick.

Jefferson leaned toward Henry Thomas. "Now, why don't you tell me why President Harrison felt the need to drag my old bones out from California? Because the last time I got a letter from Washington, it was to inform me that my commission as revoked."

Marshal Thomas gave me a quick sidelong glance. He had probably been given the impression I was in charge of the investigation, but I was ready to let Jefferson take the lead. I wanted him to take the lead. Priscilla and I had been brewing a plan since the telegram at Fort Hamilton, and Jefferson was at the center the plan.

"They sent for you because of Cold Springs, Captain Stottlemyre. Because of what you three faced down and destroyed that night." Thomas paused. "Your dismissal didn't sit right with some folks. And now, well..." He stopped, scratched the back of his neck, and sighed. "There's something out there, sir. Something I know me and my men ain't ready to face."

"Has anyone seen this *something*?" Jefferson leaned back in his chair with the blankest expression I'd ever seen on a man's face.

"No, and that's the problem. I've got whole families dead, swollen up from a dozen poisonous snake bites where there ain't any snakes, or else missing from their farmsteads. I've lost three of my deputies. Two are dead, one from the same snake bite wounds and the other decapitated. The third man went crazy. I've got a handful of legends from the local Caddo and Wichita tribes about a winged snake-god or monster living in the little hills near Hennessey Corner. That's what my madman of a deputy keeps muttering about, a giant snake with wings." Thomas gave Jefferson a sharp look. "Train and bank robbers, Comanche raiders and whiskey peddlers, those I can deal with. This is something different."

"It all sounds like tall tales and whiskey dreams, Marshal Thomas," Jefferson said.

"I know that."

Jefferson nodded. "But I've seen a tall tale in the flesh. This deputy that survived, where is he?"

"I sent him to a hospital up in Guthrie."

"What about the army?"

Marshal Widner shook his head. "They ride out on patrols from Fort Cobb every morning, annoy the settlers and local tribes, and scamper back to hide behind their walls after dark."

I watched Jefferson's eyes narrow and his hands clench. I

could tell there was going to a trip down to that fort, and woe betide the commander when Jefferson was done with him. Jefferson sat silent for several minutes. I could see him thinking hard and trying to decide how to proceed. Marshal Thomas glanced at me again, but I kept my face stone. Next to me, Priscilla fanned herself and sipped from the tea she had requested, studying the hotel lobby and watching people walking by the window as if she didn't have a care in the world.

"The way I see it," Jefferson finally said, "even if I wanted to help—and I haven't agreed yet—I don't have any authority. I'm not a U.S. Marshal anymore. I'm a police captain from San Francisco. Oklahoma Territory is a mite outside my jurisdiction."

I felt muscles I hadn't even known were tense start to relax. Jefferson was going to help.

"The federal government would give you authority, Captain Stottlemyre." Marshal Thomas reached into his coat pocket and pulled out a silver badge, gleaming in the light as if freshly minted. It was shaped like a shield and read "U.S. Special Services No. 1." Thomas set it on the table next to Jefferson's water and drew papers from a different pocket in his coat, passing them to Jefferson. I watched my old comrade read the papers and then fold them and tuck them into his own pocket. He picked up the badge and pinned it to his coat.

"I'd like to see where this is happening and talk to someone about these snake-god legends."

Marshal Thomas nodded. "I thought you might. A family named McHenry was attacked a few nights ago and...well, I'll let you see for yourself."

"We'll need a local guide," I said.

Marshal Widner nodded. "I've got a man, Trevor Halfmoon. He's a good, steady youngster. I'll arrange the loan to you of some horses, and he'll take you over to Hennessey Corner where the McHenry home was located."

"Was?" Jefferson asked.

Marshal Thomas grimaced. "Well, the buildings are still there."

Jefferson sighed and stood up. "Why don't you send your man over to meet us here? Bill and I will be ready to ride over to the McHenry place in an hour." He looked between us. "It was a long trip out from Guthrie. Where can an old man get some food in this town?"

THREE

I happily walked along next to my husband's horse. The big gray—and all the other horses for that matter—had been less than pleased with my appearance, and my William's animal had gone so far as to rear and kick before William brought him under control.

Marshal Stottlemyre, for he shall always be such to me despite any silliness of his government, kept perfect control of his own snorting and shying animal, calming it in moments, showing the horsemanship learned as a cavalry officer and frontier lawman had not diminished despite his age or time spent working the streets of San Francisco. His eyes had lit with joy the moment he swung a leg over the saddle of the paint mustang. He sat in that saddle now with an ease and grace that would be the envy of any rider from any of the world's great horse cultures.

The newest member of our little circus was a native named Trevor Halfmoon. He was a quiet young man, polite in words and soft in voice, dressed in blue denim trousers, a dark brown button down shirt, and heavy work boots. A rounded, narrow-brimmed hat rested on his head. He carried a battered revolver, an alarmingly large knife, and a Winchester rifle with brass buttons or perhaps nails inlayed in the wooden stock.

Presenting himself at the hotel as Marshal Thomas requested, there was moment of unpleasantness as the hotel manager angrily confronted Mr. Halfmoon, obviously intent on expelling him from the establishment. Marshal Stottlemyre quickly put the matter to rest with a few soft, steel covered words.

Mr. Halfmoon's horse, little more than a tan-colored pony, eyed me with suspicion when I joined the group riding out from the little village but had otherwise acted as if a large black wolf in its presence were a perfectly normal occurrence. Mr. Halfmoon had raised an eyebrow as well and subtly reached for his rifle in the saddle boot, but my William's obvious familiarity with me convinced him I was simply William's somewhat less than domesticated pet. I chuckled internally at the idea of my being domesticated in any manner.

My mirth continued as I recalled Marshal Stottlemyre and Mr. Halfmoon's reaction to dear Violet. Violet, actually Violeta Tsankova, had joined us as my maid during a particularly nasty bit of business in Bulgaria. William and I, along with agents from various countries, had dealt with a Vodnik gone completely mad. We managed to save the Tsankova family from the watery death other families were not so lucky to avoid and destroy the creature. Violeta had simply attached herself to me afterward. Our local military liaison explained that her family owed me a debt for personally rescuing their grandfather while in my wolf skin. Violeta, as the fifth of six daughters, had few prospects of her own and had been living as if she were the second son for a number of years, hunting, fishing, fighting, and working with her hands.

The Tsankova family had been insistent we take Violeta with us. We had tried to decline, but Violeta stubbornly held her ground, following us when we left, catching up to us when we thought we had outpaced her. William had shrugged as Violeta presented herself and clumsily took up the duties of my personal maid, something I had decided to go without after Cold Springs. Violeta had proved herself as a marksman and companion since, eventually learning the trade of being a lady's maid.

She stood a very normal five feet and three inches in height, with short-cropped black hair that hung loose and was cut in a sharp line in front of her eyes. Her skin was darker than my own, a deep tan in color. Violeta dressed in men's clothing: brown trousers tucked into black boots, white shirt with high collar and light tan vest, all of which fit snugly and showed her feminine form. She was not beautiful in a classical sense, but she was striking.

She spoke little English, and her dark eyes moved constantly in search of danger. She was curious about the world around her and dedicated to mine and William's security and comfort. She rode along on a heavy-shouldered mule, rifle on her back, two revolvers and a handful of daggers and small knives hanging on her belt. A short, curved-handled saber hung from the mule's saddle, and I was sure she carried explosives in her pack.

Marshal Stottlemyre had whistled low and narrowed his eyes at her when he saw the small arsenal Violeta bore. Violeta had given him a single look up and down, nodding her approval before returning to packing.

Mr. Halfmoon had reacted at her odd appearance and her obvious femininity with concerned, stating that it was not safe for a woman to travel with us when the group might face various unknown dangers. Violeta had tossed him across the stable when she gathered his intent to leave her behind because of her supposed womanly fragility. Mr. Halfmoon rose like lightning, drawing his knife with a hiss and preparing for an attack. Violeta had favored him with a smile and settled into a fighting stance of her own. For a moment it seemed there might be blood shed before we ever left Binger, but Mr. Halfmoon had laughed, sheathed his weapon, and held out a hand to Violeta, speaking in his native language as she clasped it.

I resisted the urge to dash ahead, to let my legs fly beneath me as I charged across the prairie of high fragrant grasses and red earth. It would be wonderful to run in my wolf skin, and the creature within me desired that freedom, but I worried that a local farmer or rancher fearing for the safety of his stock might decide to shoot a large black wolf. Lead bullets would not kill me, but they would hurt and perhaps force me to change. Imagine the chagrin when said rifle-wielding rancher decided to check his kill and found a wounded, naked woman instead.

The smells hit me before we reached the farmstead. Feces. Fire. Blood. Smoke. Death. Dead mammals and the musky, sharp vegetation smell I'd come to associate with snakes. And damp, dank earth. I growled despite myself, earning a sharp glance from William. The horses caught the scents a moment later and their own smells changed, becoming that of nervous sweat. I moved to the head of our column, nose down, trying to make myself look as doglike as possible. Behind me, I heard the whisper of rifles being drawn from leather saddle boots, the others reacting to my sudden change in demeanor.

We rounded a bend wrapped around a small lone hill on the trail; a track that was little more than wagon wheel ruts in the ground, and found ourselves facing what I suspected was the McHenry homestead. What none of us could have expected was the mob destroying it.

One of the barns was starting to blaze, and a good dozen men, under the direction of an older man, appeared prepared to do the same to the cabin. My survey of the situation was broken when I was forced to dodge from under the feet of Marshal Stottlemyre's horse. Behind me, William gave an oath that would have paled one of Her Majesty's veteran sailors and kicked his own animal into pursuit. I hesitated for a moment before running at full speed, keeping William's horse between me and any rifles of the mob ahead.

I drew the rifle Blenchy had loaned me from the saddle boot and urged my mount to his best sped. I was sure Blenchy would be right behind me, and if he followed my charge, then the heavily armed Violet would be chugging along behind on her mule. I had no idea what Halfmoon would do, or Lady Priscilla in wolf skin, though I suspect she would stay close to her husband, facing the danger with him. I gave the fancy rifle a glance. A gift to them from a man named Tesla, it seemed less complicated than the one Wulf had used in Cold Springs, but it was still a strange weapon. I hoped it didn't break down or misfire at a critical moment, like when a mob decided to toss an old lawman into the fire they were trying to start.

There's a saying, which means it's a damned lie, of one riot, one Ranger. Now, I've known a few Texas Rangers over the years, and while they're some of most dedicated and brave souls I've ever met, I'm not a big believer in the myth of the Rangers. Still, I hoped two old ex-U.S. Marshals, a werewolf, and a possibly crazy Bulgarian lady's maid would be enough to save the McHenry farm before the fools burned it to the ground and I lost whatever evidence might still be useful.

The crowd had the sense to part before my charge, men and women diving off to either side as I rode through them and up to the open door of the little house, I wheeled my mount around and faced the mob, rifle pointed in the air. Blenchy and Halfmoon flanked me to either side. I watched Violet guide her mule off to the left as she unslung the bolt action rifle from her shoulder and chambered a round. If it came to shooting, we had the mob in our crossfire. I caught a glimpse of the large wolf that was Lady Priscilla swing around the mob toward the back of the house, a handful of hounds barking her direction.

I gave the shocked and silent crowd a hard look. "What in the name of the creator are you people doing, burning down someone's property? You'll destroy any trace of what happened here! You people need to put away the fire and head on back to your homes."

A group of men stepped forward to face me. They looked at the badge on my jacket, then at Blenchy. "Who are you to order us around?" one of the men cried out, a short fellow dressed like a preacher or lawyer. "You aren't with the army, and you aren't a marshal."

"This ain't none of your business," called out another and there was a chorus of agreements from the mob. "You just need to ride on, mister."

This was going to go harder than I'd hoped but no worse than I'd expected. "My name is Jefferson Stottlemyre, United States Special Agent. President Harrison sent me here to Hennessey Corner on behest of Territorial Governor George Washington Steele to investigate the death and disappearances of a number of local settlers and two United States Marshals. Now, I reckon I could just start arresting— or maybe even shooting—people for destroying evidence of a possible crime, but if you all disperse and peacefully head on back to town or your homes, I don't see the need for things to get any uglier than they already are."

I watched them mill about in confusion for several seconds, and then the one who seemed to be their leader stepped up toward my horse. I rested the rifle across my saddle, pointed at the ground near the man's feet. The barn and stable were a loss, the flames spreading and consuming them, but I'd be damned if I'd let them destroy the house. He gave my strange weapon a glance before his face set like a stubborn mule. "The people of Hennessey Corner don't need any special agent from back east poking their nose into our affairs."

"Are you the town mayor? Or town marshal?" I asked quietly. "Maybe the preacher at a local church?"

"I speak for these people, if that's what you're asking, sir."

"Fair enough," I said, even though he hadn't answered my question. "Then you and the folks of Hennessey Corner need to understand that this is a federal matter now, not a local one. Whether you want it or not, there's going to be an investigation. I intend to find out what's happening here and deal with it. Now, if you have a problem with that, you're welcome to cable the territorial governor or even the office of the president himself, but if you continue to interfere with my investigation, sir, I will be forced to take action." For a moment I thought he was going to stand his ground, and I wasn't thrilled with the idea of trying to either arrest or engage in a shootout with all these people, most of whom were probably decent enough folks but frightened now and looking to lash out.

"What's going on here!" a voice called out. "What do you people think you're doing?"

I looked up to see man wearing a badge on his vest riding into the group, an elderly woman on a big black horse behind him.

"The devil's work must be dealt with," the man who spoke for the group cried out. Preacher, I decided. "We intended to purify this ground with fire. You should not interfere, Marshal."

"By burning down the whole homestead?" The marshal shook his head. "I don't know where you get your ideas, Reverend Jacob, but you and your flock need to head on home." He looked up at me. "And who might you and your bunch be?"

I nodded my greeting. "Jefferson Stottlemyre. I've been sent here to deal with a rash of disappearances and killings."

He rode up next to me, and I handed him my papers. He gave them a quick scan and handed them back. "Well, then. I suppose that means we'll be seeing each other about."

I nodded. "I hate to step all over your local authority..."

"But you're going to. Well, I think I'd rather you than Colonel Rattinger. At least you seem like a lawman and not just another big-headed fool in a uniform." He looked back at the preacher. "Jacob, I thought I told you to go home."

The preacher opened his mouth, but the elderly woman cut him off. "Do as Marshal Rich says, Jacob," she said in a quiet voice. She looked around at the milling mob. "All of you, go on home now."

There were several murmurs of "Yes, ma'am" and "Yes, Granny Creswell." I watched as the old woman rode around the people, herding them like stray cattle toward their horses and wagons, starting them back down the road, hopefully toward town. Jacob the Preacher gave me a last long angry look over his shoulder and then stomped off after them as the roof of the barn and stable collapsed.

Marshal Rich tipped his hat in our direction. "Agent Stottlemyre, come by my office when you're done here, if you want." He paused and gave Trevor Halfmoon a hard look. "Though you should know his folks aren't welcome in our town." He turned his horse and rode along behind the group, watching for stragglers and occasionally looking over his shoulder at us.

"Notice how that Marshal Rich kind of appeared out of thin air?" Blenchy said. "Like he was waiting in the wings in case someone showed up to put a stop to the mob."

"Yeah, I noticed. I also noticed how they all got docile when that Granny Creswell told them to leave, even Mr. Preacher Man." I looked at Halfmoon. "I take it the Wichita aren't welcome in Hennessey Corner?"

Halfmoon nodded. "I'm K'itaish, but yes, my people are unwelcome in their town, as are the Caddo or any tribe that fought for the Union or stayed neutral in the war." He paused. "Marshal Rich was born in South Carolina. His father was a major under General Hampton."

I nodded my understanding. Lieutenant-General Wade Hampton III was one of the great cavalry commanders of the war and one of the last southern generals to surrender.

"Is it safe to come out now?" a frightened voice, one that reminded me of my time working back in New York, called from inside the home.

Blenchy aimed his rifle at the door. "Come on out there."

A man nearly as tall and thin as Blenchy stepped out from the house, clutching a huge rig that I recognized as a bellows camera and stand. He was dressed in black trousers and coat, leather shoes, and a bowler perched on his head. "Please," he said, voice trembling. "Please, I don't mean any harm. I'm only trying to take photographs to send back to my publisher."

I peered down at him. "Are you with a newspaper or magazine, mister?"

"Nicolaas Brinkerhoff, with the *New York World*. My

publisher sent me here to capture an image of this Snake God of the Plains and get a feature article." He looked up at us, a wide smile breaking his narrow face. "Would any of you gentlemen be willing to speak about the supposed snake-monster murdering settlers on the Oklahoma prairie?"

I did my best to hide my frustration at the photographer Mr. Brinkerhoff suddenly becoming a part of our group. My suggestion that we have Halfmoon escort Brinkerhoff back to the relative safety of Binger, where he was visiting a local photographer who was giving him loan of a darkroom, was shot down. Jefferson wanted to keep him close and protect him from the folks of Hennessey Corner, who had taken exception to his photographing the McHenry homestead as part of his article for the newspaper back east.

Halfmoon and Brinkerhoff's presence meant Priscilla would need to stay in her wolf form until we returned to Binger and the privacy of the hotel. While I would have been happy to look on my beloved's face, the bigger problem was that the longer she stayed a wolf, the more the wolf took over her mind and the harder it was for her become human again.

Also, I was aggravated with Brinkerhoff because the man would not shut up. Once he was sure we weren't trying to kill him, he turned into an overly friendly, overly chatty annoyance astride a tired pony, trailing a bored mule behind him to haul all his fancy damned equipment and going on about his trip west from New York.

Brinkerhoff fell back to chat with Violet, who I was pretty sure only understood about every tenth word he said but smiled benignly and acted like she was interested. Once Brinkerhoff was busy talking to Violet, Jefferson let me know he planned to look at Brinkerhoff's photographs once they developed, hoping for evidence or some kind of clue.

I signaled Halfmoon to drop back and guard the rear as Jefferson and I followed the trail Priscilla was leading us on.

All of us had our rifles out, except Brinkerhoff, who didn't seem to be armed in any way. Pricilla's hackles had been up when she joined us at the cabin. At first I thought it was because of the ugly mob facing us, but after investigating the cabin and letting Priscilla lead us to the her own findings, we were all on edge except Brinkerhoff, who was oblivious to our danger.

There had been over a dozen dead snakes in the cabin, mostly hacked into pieces. I'd never seen the like, but at least the McHenry family gave a good account of themselves. The smell of death and decay was strong in the cabin, and I could spot the blood easy enough. The cabin window concerned me most. The shutter was smashed and part of the frame ripped out, bits of blood, hair, and cloth stuck in the wreckage. I did my bit to make sure the house remained untouched after we left. I wished my old Granny Coulton had been there to give this family strong protections *before* the monster came and wondered if even granny's hex magic would have been enough.

In the yard, Halfmoon found enough fired cartridges to tell us someone had emptied a rifle. We couldn't get any tracks around the house because of the mob, and the barn was burned to the ground, all the dead animals inside lost. Priscilla, through a series of yips, short barks, and whines, lead us behind the house. We found an old Colt Navy, fired twice, a child's doll made of rags, and the bloated body of a hound, flies buzzing around it. The poor creature was covered in snake bites. We found the first footprint there.

The print reminded me a little bit of those left by chuckwalla lizards in the Arizona desert, except those lizards didn't walk on two legs, and this thing must have been about five times my weight, with a stride half again as long as any man I'd ever tracked. A big, two-legged lizard. Dear God. I hoped that rifle I'd given Jefferson would work against it, because that farmer's rifle hadn't seemed to help him. I was really tired of monsters I couldn't kill with lead.

I was also tired of watching Priscilla in her furry form. I

wanted to look at her face, touch her skin. I wanted her with me when I faced down this giant lizard. And I wanted that damned photographer gone; I could tell he was going to be less than useless, and I didn't want one of us getting killed trying to keep the idiot out of trouble. I wasn't even sure he would have the sense to run; in fact, I was afraid he'd freeze like a frightened rabbit.

We were a half mile from the McHenry farm and I reckoned about two miles from the town of Hennessey Corner when we can upon both the hill and small squadron of cavalry at the same time. Priscilla had stopped on the trail, ears up and trying to look more like a particularly wild dog than, say, a huge black wolf. Jefferson rode forward to meet the men in blue. He spoke the language of soldiers, so I turned most of my attention to the hill Priscilla had been leading us toward.

The tower of red stone and dirt jutting up from the land, surrounded at its base by elms, oaks, and a few pines. I'd guess about eighty to ninety feet tall and maybe two, two hundred and fifty feet round. Flat at the top with a ridge partway down, it was really more of a small, lonely butte.

"Crying Woman Mound," Halfmoon said softly. "This is a…place to avoid."

I tossed him a sharp look, keeping one ear on the conversation Jefferson was having with the cavalry officer, a young captain, little more than a boy from the looks of him. A gray-whiskered sergeant sat on his horse near the captain. "Oh?" I asked.

"Yes. When we return to town, I will tell you more." Halfmoon licked his lips. "I had hoped, but…"

"You there," the dark-haired captain called out, kicking his horse and heading toward us. Jefferson turned his mustang to pursue as the old sergeant shook his head. "Who are you? To which tribe do you belong?"

I moved between the captain and Halfmoon. The cavalry officer pulled up short, as if surprised at being challenged in any way. His pulled himself together in a moment, puffing up in his uniform. "I asked you a question."

"Here now, Captain Haskell," Jefferson said, riding up. "Mr. Halfmoon is our hired guide." Jefferson moved his horse next to mine, helping shield Halfmoon. The rest of the cavalry troop began to fan out behind the sergeant as he walked his horse over to join us. Most of them were little more than boys, but I spotted a couple of troopers who looked steady, older, steel-eyed. I hoped the captain didn't want to make things difficult for us. Priscilla slunk in among our horses and settled next to Violet's mule. Mr. Brinkerhoff asked Violet what was happening in a too-loud whisper. I heard Violet mutter, "Trouble."

"I must insist, Agent Stottlemyre. Colonel Rattinger has made it a mission to rid the area of the incessant drumming the local tribes insist on engaging in every fall. It frightens the settlers, and it must come to a stop. I'm to question any Indian I encounter and bring them back to the stockade if I feel they are being uncooperative. I must insist, sir."

Halfmoon straightened in his saddle and guided his mount between mine and Jefferson's. "I am Trevor Halfmoon, oldest son of Lieutenant Adam Halfmoon, who fought with the First Kansas Volunteers. I live near Binger and work on my parent's farm."

The captain looked surprised, as if he had no idea anyone but a white man might have fought for the Union Army, little less have been an officer. Somebody needed to start teaching some history to the youngsters. Such ignorance was a woeful thing indeed.

Jefferson frowned. "As I said, Mr. Halfmoon is our hired guide and so an employee of the federal government."

Captain Haskell frowned. "And you know nothing of the drummers who meet here each year?"

"No, sir."

I could hear the lie in Halfmoon's voice. There was a subtle shift in the saddle, a nervous twitch of one hand. He looked down as he spoke, as if in deference and submission. Halfmoon knew something, had told me as much before the captain came charging over. Jefferson and I would need to have a serious talk with him.

"I'd love to get a photograph of the hill," Brinkerhoff suddenly said, climbing down from his horse and handing the reins to Violet. He looked at the troop of cavalry. "Would you chaps be willing to pose for a photograph? The readers back east would love a look at our brave men taming the west and protecting innocent settlers from the dangers of the wilds."

The effect was dramatic and immediate. The young captain swelled with pride, and within moments his sergeant had arrayed the troopers in front of the mound to Brinkerhoff's satisfaction, all thoughts of harassing Halfmoon forgotten. Brinkerhoff set up his equipment efficiently and took a few photographs, directing the soldiers to various locations. Through it all Jefferson sat astride his horse, amusement on his face, and I had to wonder if the damned photographer had somehow known he was going to defuse our little standoff. I shook my head, thinking I was probably giving the man too much credit.

After about an hour by my reckoning, Brinkerhoff declared satisfaction. The captain shook hands with the photographer and then Jefferson, who told the youngster we would be calling on his commanding officer in the coming days to discuss the crisis. The sergeant called the men into formation, and the whole shebang rode south at a quick trot, no doubt wanting to be safely behind their stockade walls before the sunset. I looked at the sun getting lower in the sky and wondered what kind of danger would make an entire cavalry troop scurry for shelter.

When the troop was a good two hundred yards away, Jefferson nodded to Brinkerhoff, who was packing up his equipment, and Violet, who still held the reins to Brinkerhoff's horse. "You two stay here for now. Bill and I are going to go take a ride around the hill." He looked at Trevor Halfmoon. "Are you with us? I won't make you come along if you don't want."

The young man's face set in a grim frown. "The truth is, there *should* be drumming here. For time beyond memory, no matter which tribe or clan dwelled here, there was always drumming through the late harvest."

"Why?" Jefferson asked.

Halfmoon pointed to Crying Woman Mound. "To bind that which dwells within. It nearly escaped once. When the gold-craving Spanish swept through, one of their Mage-Priests weakened the bindings on the mound, and the monster slipped into our world. The other Spanish priests joined with the five clans, their magic driving the Snake-God back into the hill. The Spanish soldiers melted down their own arms and armor to forge the iron and steel door sealing the rip between the worlds."

More magic. Wonderful. I looked over at Jefferson. His face was almost blank, thinking hard about our next move. "Okay. We scout the place and then head back to Binger. I don't want be out here with us exposed any longer than needed. We give it a look and then head out, get the civilians to safety."

He was looking at me when he spoke, and I could read that he wanted to leave both Brinkerhoff and Halfmoon behind when we returned. He would probably try to leave Priscilla and Violet as well, but I already knew the futility of that argument. Priscilla and I were full partners, and Violet wouldn't let Priscilla go into danger without her.

We rode around the hill three times. Priscilla followed the track of the giant snake, but it just vanished at the side of the hill. It was like the creature had slipped through the red rock of the hill. We did find a woman's shoe and more bits of torn clothing, but no sign of the McHenrys or any other local folks. The local rattlers, king snakes, and other small reptiles seemed to consider the hill their home, and we had a time not stepping on any of them. The snakes watched us, but even the normally aggressive diamondbacks stayed still at our passing. We rode back in silence, collecting Brinkerhoff and Violet. Heading toward Binger, I had a feeling I wouldn't get to sleep in a warm bed next to Priscilla tonight. The three riders we picked up as we passed north of Hennessey Corner, who spent the entire trip to Binger shadowing us, did nothing to ease my worries.

FOUR

"It had to be a snake," Blenchy said. "I hate snakes."

"A snake god," Lady Priscilla pointed out. She gave Blenchy a small smile as we rode through the darkness toward Crying Woman Mound. I would have thought she'd want to stay a wolf for this, but she had simply shrugged when I asked. Blenchy told me as we waited for Lady Priscilla and her maid to finish preparing back at the hotel that the longer she stayed in her wolf-skin the harder it was for her to transition back. I could hear the worry in his voice, worry that someday the pull of the wild creature would become too strong, the call to stay a wolf would overwhelm her human mind, and Lady Priscilla Talbot would vanish.

"Alright then, a terrible big snake," Blenchy finally muttered.

I chuckled despite our situation. "Good to see you still have a sense of humor, Bill." He gave me a dark look, and all I could do was smile in return. I didn't completely understand, but being back in a saddle, under the stars—I felt alive. And if there were a monster or god waiting for us at this mound, then I hoped the rifle I carried would be useful.

Trevor Halfmoon had explained the legend of the winged snake-god, a creature the native peoples of this land had worked to appease and contain for so long that truth and myth were indistinguishable. The harvest-time drumming was part of the ritual but had apparently been disrupted by the cavalry. Lady Priscilla spoke softly of other ancient snake gods as we rode, though where she had managed to learn all this lore or keep it straight in her head was a beyond me. Snake-god myths were common enough, she said, from malevolent Set of the Egyptians to the winged Quetzalcoatl, who had been worshipped for centuries in lands not far from here. There were rumors of an even darker serpent deity, one

that moved between worlds, manifesting in much the manner
Halfmoon described. A giant monster: snakelike in a human
body, with wings and two legs, sharp claws on the end of
hands the size of dinner plates, and fangs dripping with
venom. It was the kind of stuff to cause nightmares, except
I'd been having those for two years now.

At the moment, I was more worried by the riders who
had been tracking us since we had left Crying Woman Mound
earlier in the evening. They always stayed just too far away for
me to get a good look at them, but for a moment I thought
one might have been the crazy man preaching end times
when I arrived in Binger. One thing was for sure: they want
us to know we were being watched. I glanced toward the last
position they had been at, but no one was in sight now.
Maybe the encroaching darkness had sent them scurrying
back to their homes. I could hope.

"It just stops," Blenchy said, disbelief plain in his voice.
He was staring at the side of the mound, where Lady Priscilla
had found the end of the giant snake-lizard tracks after the
cavalry had ridden away.

"You always act surprised. I told you it ended here."
Lady Priscilla's voice had a note of annoyance, one Blenchy
picked up right quick.

"Sorry, darling. I know you're good at what you do, and
I know you said the trail ended right in the middle of the hill,
but seeing it for myself." He shook his head. "You'd think
nothing much would surprise me anymore, but still."

"We're sure it didn't climb up to the top?" I asked.

"No," Blenchy and Lady Priscilla said together. They
shared a quick smile before she took over the conversation.
"It appears to have walked into the side of the hill."

"Magic," Violet muttered, the word sounding like a curse
falling from her lips, and perhaps it was. "Always the magic."

"What do you think about setting up camp over on the
patch of flat ground between the trees? We'd be able to watch
the hill," Blenchy said.

"And then move in the middle of the night and cold camp over inside that stand of oaks there about fifty yards on?" I gestured to the spot.

Blenchy nodded. "I like it. We'd be able to keep an eye on this hill and catch anyone approaching the old camp, with a little luck."

"I don't much believe in luck," I told him.

Blenchy chuckled. "I've found I trust it more these days." He took his pack and bedroll from the back of his saddle. "Priscilla and I'll set up the warm camp and get food started, if that's okay with you."

Violet and I took care of the animals, unsaddling them, checking backs, legs, mouths, and hoofs, rubbing them down and brushing them before setting them in a picket with feed bought in Binger and carried for the overnight trip. We planned to have the animals back in the stable by midday tomorrow. Violet and I carried our rifles back to the temporary camp and settled on the ground. We heated a meal brought from the hotel eatery over the small fire. Blenchy made strong black coffee and leaned back to read from a battered copy of Dumas by the light of the flames. It was enough to lull a man into complacency.

It was a testament to the life my friends must live that they all managed to vanish into the darkness at the first crack of the rifle and smash of the bullet into the tin cup I had just set aside. I was a little slower but changed position before the second shot, moving away from the light and putting a tree between me and where I guessed the shooter was. I blinked a few times to help my eyes adjust. To my left I heard soft footfalls fade into the night. There was a low growl.

"You alright?" Blenchy whispered.

"Yup. Expect for my pride." I worked the bolt action on my new rifle. The weapon gave a soft whine as I watched the darkness for movement or muzzle flashes. "I must be getting old, Bill. I knew we were in enemy territory, but I let my damned guard down. We should've started with a cold camp. I should've known they'd try to ambush us."

"We both thought they'd try after we'd bunked down for the night. Priscilla went to scout them. Violet's about twenty yards away, up in a tree."

Our unseen attackers fired into the camp again, kicking up dirt near the coffeepot and knocking it over. To my left came the roar of Violet using her Turkish Mauser, the heavy infantry rifle spitting fire into the night and lighting up the tree she hide in. I heard swearing from where I'd seen the muzzle flash up the hill and wondered if Violet had scored a hit in the darkness.

There was a high, wild howling that made the hairs on my arms and neck stand up. Even as a part of my brain reasoned it must be Lady Priscilla, another, more primitive part of me wanted to flee. The horses, which had been relatively quiet until now except for some soft nickering and stomping, snorted and pulled at the picket line, the mule letting off an alarmed bray. Hoof-beats retreated down the hill, heading away. I let out a relieved sigh, relaxing the tiniest bit.

Lady Priscilla the wolf came running into view, low to the ground, mouth hanging open, teeth gleaming. Behind her, the hill started to slither toward us.

"The horses!" Blenchy cried out.

I broke cover and ran after him. Lady Priscilla stopped near the fire and turned, head low and growling, snapping at a pair of snakes. I heard Violet jump down from the tree. Blenchy beat me to the animals, all of them panicked and nearly impossible to control. Another warming growl came from Lady Priscilla as the first wave of snakes overran the camp.

Violet pulled a flaming brand from the campfire, waving it to protect her lady. Blenchy smashed down with the butt of his Sharps rifle, using it like a club, but there too many of them. I gained control of the mustang and swung up on the bare back of the little horse as the others, eyes rolling in terror and nostrils flaring, ran into the night. Clutching the lead for the mule, who had kept his head better than the horses, I kicked my mustang, making the poor beast jumped toward the fire. Blenchy bodily flung Lady Priscilla, naked, human, and with blood running down her leg, onto the back of the mule and climbed up after her while still striking snakes with his rifle.

Violet cried out a word I didn't understand, pointing wide-eyed at the hill. She shook off whatever fear or shock gripped her and, rifle slung over her shoulder, ran toward me.

It was a large black form, bat-like wings on its back. It leapt down, wings opening as it glided, wicked talons on its hands flexing in anticipation of rending its intended victims. Tossing the lead for the mule to Blenchy, I tightened my legs around the mustang, lifted the rifle to my shoulder, and squeezed the trigger as Violet climbed up on the mustang with me.

The Tesla rifle was similar in body to Violet's Mauser: a dark wooden stock, metal barrel and mechanism, bolt action instead of the familiar lever of a Winchester. The box magazine didn't have standard cartridges but a copper casing with a flat top of silver. When I asked Blenchy what it fired, he smiled and said I should see for myself. We only had twenty rounds of ammunition, so I'd been loath to use it. Now seemed like the appropriate time.

There was a soft popping noise, and the rifle gave no kick. The only physical sign that I had fired the weapon was the small, green, glowing light that shot from the end of the barrel like a tiny star streaking toward what I supposed was the snake god. I watched over the barrel as the green light struck true, hitting the thing squarely in the chest.

The entire area lit up in a wave of eerie green as the bullet of light exploded against the monster. I caught a glimpse of the thing as it threw back its shoulders and flapped its wings, then the mustang decided he'd had enough and raced off into the night with me astride and hanging on for dear life. I lay myself flat, felt another warm body resting against my back and heard a woman's voice muttering invectives in a language I didn't understand. I glanced over my shoulder to find Violet had managed to hang on. Good. It meant I didn't have to go back for her. I checked for pursuit from the monster and found none. I couldn't see Blenchy and Lady Priscilla. I had to hope they were safe. In the distance, I heard the faint sound of drums.

With no real way to control the horse, I clung to its back and mane while trying to hang onto my rifle. Violet had a death grip on my middle, so if one of us fell, we both fell. All I could do was let the animal have its head and run until it decided it was safe. After fifteen minutes and a couple of heart-stopping, back-wrenching turns, we came upon a dirt track and then a small cluster of houses. It wasn't Binger, and we had gone the wrong way for Fort Cobb. The horse has found its way to Hennessey Corner, which didn't surprise me at all. It must have made the trip between the two towns before. What did surprise me was that we were right behind the mule. Blenchy, clutching Lady Priscilla close, drew his Colt and fired into the air as the mule stopped walking. Our horse, blowing hard, came to a shaking halt.

Violet vaulted off the horse and was at Blenchy's feet in an instant. He waved her off and, carrying the still-naked Lady Priscilla cradled in his arms, started toward the town's crossroads, obviously looking for a doctor or any help among the handful of businesses on the street. His shot had woken up the local dogs, most of which began to bark and howl. Lights came on, and within minutes the townsfolk, most in their night clothes, began to rush into the street. I heard Blenchy calling for a doctor and the entire mob swooped them up and started toward one of the houses.

"What the hell happened?" I turned toward the voice. Marshal Rich had his trousers and boots on, gun belted to his waist and suspenders over his red undershirt. "Agent Stottlemyre, what happened?"

I had to stop and think about what to tell the man. I watch as my three companions vanished into a white wood framed two-story house. "We ran into a bit of trouble out by

Crying Woman. Someone took a couple of shots at us and then…well, we ran into some mighty odd-acting snakes."

"Damn." He took a couple of deep breaths and nodded. "Let's get over to Granny Creswell's and see how your folks are, and then we need to talk, I think."

Marshal Rich lead me to the house where the crowd had guided Blenchy. The crowd of townspeople, solemn and silent, parted before us. I held my rifle over my shoulder, pointed toward the sky. I hadn't set the safety on the unfamiliar weapon, and I knew I had a round chambered. I touched my Schofield as what seemed like a dozen people favored me with dark, malevolent stares.

Blenchy was in the front parlor, a room with cushioned sitting chairs, dark wood tables, and a handful of paintings and tintypes on the walls. The wallpaper was pale blue flowers on a white background. The room was lit by a three large lamps. Blenchy held his hat in his hands, his rifle resting in a corner.

"Priscilla?" I asked.

"Violet and Mrs. Creswell took her upstairs. A couple of local women are up there with them. The girl they sent down said the bites weren't deep and they should be able to draw out any poison. That's all I…" He swallowed, and I could see the anguish and fear in his eyes.

"Why don't we head over to my office?" Marshal Rich said softly. "You two can tell me what happened, and I'll get you both some coffee. We can be back here in a minute if there's news." He placed a hand on Blenchy's shoulder. "I trust Granny Creswell to handle a snake bite more that I would Doc Meaghan over in Binger and a damned lot more than that army surgeon over at the fort."

Blenchy looked ready to rebel, and I couldn't blame him. I had a feeling we shouldn't let the Marshal split us up. Something about the way the locals hung around outside Granny Creswell's porch and the way Rich was trying to firmly but gently steer us toward the jail worried me. Still, I figured Lady Priscilla would be safe enough with Violet here to watch over her, and if Lady Priscilla wasn't too badly injured she could turn into a wolf and fight free or flee from the women watching her. I didn't want whatever Rich had planned to happen in this house, surrounded as it was by the growing mob. The jail might not be any better, and it was a risk leaving Lady Priscilla here, but I knew something was up, and if I could let it happen quietly, maybe I could handle it. I caught Blenchy's eye and gave him a nod.

He frowned, glanced up the stairs, and took up his rifle. "Okay," he said softly, and I knew he was on guard for trouble.

Marshal Rich nodded. "You, Emmett," he said to a boy on the porch. "You wait here until Granny Creswell or one of the women comes down. Tell them where to find these gentlemen, and run me any message they might have. You understand?"

The boy nodded.

I followed Marshal Rich and Blenchy, bringing up the rear as we exited Granny Creswell's. There were still several men milling about, including Preacher Jacob. I set the safety on the rifle and slipped the leather tie-down from the hammer of my pistol. The group of men followed up the street toward the little square building on the southwest corner of the two crossed streets that was obviously the jail.

Once inside, Marshal Rich settled behind his desk as Blenchy and I arrayed ourselves across from him. A couple of the men followed us, blocking the only door out of the building. I noted the revolver on the desk, next to a tin cup and a large notebook.

"Now then, gentlemen," Marshal Rich said, "why don't you tell me what happened to that woman out there?" He picked up the revolver and cocked the hammer in one swift, smooth motion. "And I'm afraid I need your weapons, gents. I don't know what you two have done, but I reckon anytime I see a woman naked and bleeding, I should assume the worst. Hand over your guns nice and slow."

###

It was the shock of the bite that forced me from wolf to woman.

At the first shot, Violeta and I dove for cover. I've made quickly disrobing a bit of science, and clever Violeta had helped modifying my garments so I could dress in the current fashion of a respectable woman but be undressed and running in moments. It was a necessary skill in our profession. So it was that I was making a circuit of the dark hill in minutes, seeking the position of those who attacked us.

I caught their scent: three men, unwashed and satiated on alcohol. One swore and admonished what appeared to be the youngest, holding a long rifle similar to William's, to keep trying to "drive the damned coyotes from the gold." The third was silent, watching our camp with a spyglass. There was quick exchange of rifle fire with my companions. I howled and started back down the hill, heading toward our camp with my gathered information to pass to William and Marshal Stottlemyre.

It appeared from the hill a dozen paces in front of me, though appeared is perhaps too tame a word. It more emerged from the hill, bending the darkness about its almost two-dimensional form. For several moments I stood, transfixed, watching as the flat form separated from the red rock, became three-dimensional. It extended its leathery wings in a short flap, crouched, and hissed with a forked tongue testing the air, wicked talons on its hands flexing and red snake eyes staring malevolently toward our camp. Around legs as thick as sturdy logs came the slithering form of over a dozen snakes, a dozen more following as they started down the hill, covering the ground so suddenly that I thought them summoned. Perhaps they were summoned, I realized.

My hackles rose as the predator inside of me took control, breaking me from the fascinated trance I had fallen into. The monster turned its red eyes toward me, and they

43

were an abyss which promised only the escape of death. I howled in fear before I fled the living horror.

The snakes rose up from near our campfire as if sprouting from the very earth under my paws. I had thought all of them behind me, but one reared and bit me on the shoulder and two on the legs. I stumbled, the pain flooding my body as I rolled away from the bright campfire. The shock stunned the wolf, and I immediately switched back to woman. A fourth snake, rattling its anger, latched onto my hip.

The next several minutes passed in a blur. I have a vague recollection of being lifted onto the back of the mule, a glimpse of Violeta's pale face as she wielded a flaming log. Screams and shots followed by a rough, bouncy ride through the night. William whispering in my ear that everything would be all right as he exhorted our mount to greater speed. The loud report of a gun; being carried into a building with too many bright lights and too many sharp smells; a soft bed and hands exploring my body as Violeta whispered and sobbed in her native language nearby. Sharp odors filling my nose as my body was dressed in a gown. An elderly woman who smelled of dirt and death giving orders as fever gripped my sweating body.

Then the room was cleared, and I was left alone with the sharp scents and Violeta, who was wiping my brow with a cool, damp cloth. "Change," she whispered. "The others, they have gone. Change, mistress. It is safe. Violeta will protect you."

The poison flowed in my veins, befuddling my thoughts, but I latched onto Violeta's words. They were wise. I called the beast within as Violeta once more urged me to change my form. I had used this trick in the past, to heal injuries, the change from woman to wolf to woman making me whole. I shifted down to the wolf, just for a minute, just long enough to neutralize the snake venom killing me. I shifted back, becoming my normal self while Violeta adjusted the nightgown to fit my limbs once more before motioning me to silence. Closing my eyes, I heard the soft voices approach and the door to the room open.

"She ain't dead yet." A woman's voice. She sounded disappointed. "She even looks a little better."

"No, she hasn't died." The older woman, the one who smelled of dirt and death. "But she won't last long, I think. Sometimes when poisoned, the body stops fighting. She might look quite peaceful before she's gone." She paused. "Girl, how is your lady?"

Violeta replied in her native Slavic tongue. She sounded as if she were asking questions and had pitched her voice to be more like a little girl's. I felt the damp rag on my brow.

"What'll we do with her?" the first voice asked. "She's armed like a Comanche raider."

"She'll be easy enough to deal with, I think. He will need tender flesh, and no one will miss her. There's been too much attention brought on by his feedings."

"It's a wonder the cavalry hasn't blundered onto something through sheer luck," the first voice said.

"True," the one who smelled like dirt answered. "Ned's dealing with the men. He's taken them to the jail to arrest them for assaulting this one. Once he has their weapons…things will go back to quiet soon enough. Just one more midnight and He will rise."

I could feel my strength returning as I rested on the bed. If these strange women, all the strange villagers in fact, thought to deal easily with us, they were in for a surprise. Violeta pressed softly on my head as my muscles tensed.

"I need to go pull a bullet out of the idiot Tesch boy."

"What were Zeke and his brothers doing out at the mound tonight?"

"Searching for the Spanish gold and tangling with our meddlers. I've told them young fools time and again there isn't any Spanish gold. I'm tempted to let the Children bite one of them."

"You want me to stay here and watch these two, Granny?"

"Yes. The woman should die soon enough. Pretend to comfort her maid when she passes. If the girl gets too hysterical, give her a cup of the tea with valerian. That will keep her calm until I get done with the Tesch boy."

I listened to both women step out of the room. At the click of the door, I opened my eyes and sat up. "Violeta, I need clothes, quickly. We have to reach the jail."

She nodded and slipped out the door of the room. I stood and stretched, warming tense muscles and checking myself for injuries. My body had accumulated innumerable scars since my first change, and tonight's events had added a few more, it seemed. Confident in Violeta's ability to procure garments, I dropped the borrowed nightgown to the floor and washed in the basin of water on the dresser. I spun as the door opened. If someone other than Violeta entered the room, I would deal with them without remorse or mercy. Violeta backed into the room, dragging a woman with her. She tossed the unconscious woman onto the bed and began to efficiently undress her. The woman was alive, I was relieved to find, and close enough to my size to allow her clothing to work for my purposes. I dressed quickly as Violeta caught me up on everything she knew.

We were in the home of Granny Creswell, the woman who smelled of dirt and death to my wolf. Violeta had noted that everyone in the village seemed to defer to the old woman. She reiterated what I had heard about Marshal Stottlemyre and William being arrested for assaulting me in the wilds. She had overheard Granny Creswell tell a woman named Clara to "gather the others." One of the women sent a teenage boy to find Pastor Jacob with instructions for him to gather other men and go to the jail. It sounded like a mob was forming. Again.

"People talk when they think I do not understand," Violeta said.

"Your English seems much improved," I noted as we tied the woman to the bed.

"Yes. I listen to you and I learn."

"Excellent."

We left the house unchallenged, Violeta taking up her rifle from where it was propped up in the corner of the parlor. She led me outside where the mule and horse were tied to a rail. Her revolvers and sword hung from the mule's saddle and she took up both, buckling them on before handing me a revolver. I watched as she pulled a wicked-looking bayonet from her pack and affixed it to her already impressive rifle. Violeta took the leads for the horse and mule, walking behind me as I set a brisk pace down the dirt street.

The jail was simple to find. All we had to do was follow the voices. In moments we spotted a mob of angry men milling menacingly about a low, square, stone building. I glanced over my shoulder to find Violeta tying the animals to a post in front of a large wooden building, the sign on the false front proclaiming it "T.A. Milner and Sons Dry Goods." She caught up to me at a trot.

The crowed of men made a low buzzing noise, as if their voices were those of a swarm of bees primed to attack. I shouldered past the first knotted group of five before someone made to stop me. A man in a brown suit, hatless and beardless, gripped my arm as I tried to pass. "Here now, miss. This is no business for a lady."

"My fiancé's safety is my business, and I would thank you to release my arm, sir."

The gentleman hesitated too long for my comfort, and I suppose for Violeta's comfort as well. With a grunt and whoosh of breath, he doubled over as Violeta drove the butt of her rifle into his stomach. Another man moved to intercept us. Violeta snapped her rifle around and placed the point of her bayonet under his throat.

I lifted my weapon and drew back the hammer. "Gentlemen, if you please, I have business with your Marshal Rich." I allowed a bit of the predator to come forward as I spoke, enough to give me an aura of menace without any manifestation. The crowd quieted and parted before me. I felt

Violeta move to cover my back. I pushed past the two men guarding the door. They parted in surprise as I forced my way in, grunting a quick "ma'am" each as they took off their hats. Secure in the knowledge that Violeta would protect me from behind, I focused on the scene before me.

Marshal Rich, his face flushed and angry, held a pistol in his right hand, hammer drawn back, ready to fire. Marshal Stottlemyre faced Rich, a deep frown on his otherwise calm face, his hands resting loose near his own weapon, still holstered. William had turned to face the two men at the door, his rifle on his shoulder. I knew from experience how quickly he could lower his weapon and fire. The rifle was a single-shot, so his plan would be to charge behind the bullet. The entire tableau was set for sudden violence, and the air reeked with anger and sweat. I wondered how long they had been engaged in this standoff.

All of them stopped arguing and turned their attention toward me. Good. It saved me doing something vulgar, like whistling. "Marshal Rich, may I have a word?"

The man's jaw tightened, and his clenched mouth worked on something unseen for several seconds. The weapon in his hand, still aimed at Marshal Stottlemyre, wavered ever so slightly. "Miss—"

"Lady," I corrected him. "Lady Priscilla Ann Talbot, daughter of the Fifth Earl of Winston, thank you. Now, please explain why you are holding a weapon on my friend while these two gentlemen are threatening my intended?"

Rich cleared his throat. "I wanted… I mean, I thought…." He frowned. "I was arresting them for assaulting you, ma'am."

"Oh. Well, I can assure you neither of these fine gentlemen has assaulted me, sir. Though I suppose I could understand your confusion."

He narrowed his eyes. "Well, they did bring you into town unconscious, naked, and bloody. What was I supposed to think?" He placed the hammer on his gun down and set the weapon on his desk. He took up a placating and apologetic attitude. "You seem much improved, ma'am."

"Yes."

"And dressed."

"One of your local ladies kindly provided for me, for which I am grateful." I paused for effect. "May we leave now? It has been a trying night, and I want a bath and bed. We have rooms in Binger, and I would like to return to them."

"I—well—ma'am." Marshal Rich was grasping for any reason to detain us, but my appearance had both figuratively and literally disarmed him.

"Between being ambushed by shadowy figures and attacked by oddly behaved snakes, I would prefer my own bed tonight." Outside, I heard the sounds of someone being sick to his stomach, no doubt the unlucky fellow Violeta had clubbed with her rifle. "As you can see, I am uninjured, and there is no need for your concern. May we leave?" I asked again. I wanted out of Hennessey Corner. There was no telling how long the owner of my borrowed clothing would remain undiscovered or unconscious.

The Marshal hesitated for a moment and seemed to deflate in his chair. "Go on then, all of you."

The crowd murmured angrily as we emerged from the jail alive, unmolested, and with our freedom, robbing them of any reason to break into the violence they seemed to desire, though Preacher Jacob did offer a diatribe about sin and demons, and he may have called me a scarlet woman. William and Marshal Stottlemyre stayed silent and wary as we left, ready to spring into action while trying to avoid inciting conflict. We rode away from Hennessey Corner on our two remaining animals, subdued but with as much dignity as we could manage. Violeta and I passed along our new information to William and the Marshal. The ride was slow and cold but mercifully without pursuit by angry villagers, snake-gods, or any other threat. A mile out of Hennessey Corner I dismounted, disrobed, and changed to my wolf, allowing the mule to move faster. I left my borrowed clothing tied to a fence. Let the people of Hennessey Corner make of that what they would.

We entered the sleeping village of Binger to a handful of desolate barks from local dogs, all of whom slunk away when I growled in answer. William and Violeta smuggled me into our rooms, where I changed. I wondered if I could get a bath. I turned to find a worried look on William's face as he regarded my naked body. Banishing Violeta to her small room, I did everything within my power to reassure my love I was whole and healthy.

FIVE

"Damn it, Bill, stop whistling."

The two of us had ridden back to the location of last night's camp, leaving Lady Priscilla behind to relax for the day. She had been through the roughest patch of us all during last night's violence and had earned the right to sleep in. Violet had stayed behind as well, tending and guarding Lady Priscilla while she rested. They planned to visit the photographer Brinkerhoff later in the day.

Luck had been with us, and the horses that had run off last night made their way back to the stables on their own. It saved me from explaining their loss to both the stable owner and Marshal Widner and allowed us to retrieve some of our gear.

It had been good to sleep in a bed last night, though a man could wish the walls were a little thicker and his neighbors a little less enthusiastic. My glares at them both over breakfast in the hotel had gone either unnoticed or ignored, the two paying attention to each other in a quiet, gentle way. I couldn't fault them, of course. I just missed my own wife.

After we finished eating, Blenchy and Lady Priscilla went back to their rooms while I walked down to the telegraph office. I paid for my messages, left instructions on how and who to contact with the replies and then walked about town a bit. I stopped by the photographer's home, but it was locked, and there was no sign of Brinkerhoff or his host. Checking in with Marshal Widner, the man shook his head at my description of the previous night's events and allowed that the people of Hennessey Corner were a strange bunch, in his estimation. He warned me that the oldest Tesch boy, Hank, would probably be around, preaching his end times vitriol. Widner asked me if I wanted him arrested, but I declined, instead stopping to listen to the young man spewing his message of doom. He was definitely one of the riders who had followed us yesterday. He kept glaring at me as he spoke. I tipped my hat to him and strolled back to the hotel.

"Sorry, Jefferson. I'm just feeling how grand it is to be alive." Blenchy tossed me a sly look as he gathered up the remains of the cooking equipment. My cup was a loss; a bullet had passed clean through, leaving huge holes.

"I'm surprised Priscilla had any energy for such things."

The grin on his face widened. "I had no idea the walls were so thin. I'd take it as a favor if you didn't tell Priscilla. She'd be right mortified. I promise we'll be more discreet in the future."

"Discreet. Quieter. I promise I won't tell her." I was trying not to think about it anymore. "At least you get to bring her along on this disaster."

"She turns into a giant black wolf."

"Well, there is that." I scanned the red rock hill for trouble, rifle at the ready. It was peaceful and beautiful today, hardly the place a fellow would expect a giant snake-god and his slithering minions to explode from. Blenchy and I both looked, but we couldn't even find any tracks. Except for the shattered remains of our camp, no one would know last night's fight and flight had happened.

After packing our gear, we scouted around a bit and found the spot where our ambushers had hidden, including dried blood on a pile of fallen sugar maple leaves. Violet had hit one of them for sure. We followed a trail down the far side of the hill, past an abandoned and burned-out homestead.

"I think this is the Foster place," Blenchy said.

We rode around it, but it was obvious the townsfolk of Hennessey Corner had done here what they'd tried to at the McHenry farm. I wondered if they'd gone back and finished the job after we left. I wouldn't be surprised. We turned out horses south, toward Fort Cobb.

Located on the west wide of Cobb Creek, the fort rested on high ground backed by a sandy hill about a mile east of the town of the same name, a dusty place not unlike Binger. The fort's construction was wooden pickets and adobe clay. The walls of most of the buildings and barracks were wood. The flag on the central pole hung listlessly in the still air.

The fort had changed hands between Union and Confederate forces a couple of times during the war and had seen its fair share of fighting. I knew it was slowly being abandoned in favor of the new Camp Wichita thirty of so miles further south. At one time Fort Cobb had boasted three companies of cavalry and one of infantry. One bare company of cavalry, a hundred or so men, remained at the post.

We rode in between two stables, stopping to speak with a bewhiskered sergeant who rushed up to challenge us. I identified myself, and he pointed towards the cluster of three adobe brick and sandstone buildings across the parade grounds where the creek flowed into the fort. He fell into step next to us, an escort to the commander's office. A squad of twenty or so troopers, led by the young Captain, rode past us and onto the trail leading north. We stopped in front of the post commander's office and dismounted, tying the horses up to the rail in front of the sandstone building. The sergeant knocked on the door, and a gruff baritone voice called for us to enter. The sergeant opened the door, giving me the long-suffering look that only a senior sergeant can muster.

The post commander's office was in the front of what I suspected were his quarters. A desk, a couple of chairs, and three lanterns were the sparse furnishings. There were maps with patrol routes nailed to the walls and a pile of letters and telegraph dispatches on the desk. A picture of President Harrison hung on the wall. The man's hat and weapons hung from a peg behind the desk.

Colonel Rattinger sat behind the desk, dressed in his full uniform. He was mostly bald, except for a ring of hair low on his head running from ear to ear. His beard was neatly trimmed. I figured he would be fairly short, maybe no taller than five and half feet. He narrowed his eyes as he took in my badge, holding what looked like a crumpled telegraph message in his hands.

I had to wonder who this full colonel had crossed to end up with such a miserable posting. With only a company of soldiers and decommissioning of the fort coming, there should have been no more than a major in command, probably no more than the young captain. From what little I'd heard during my briefing in Binger and my observations of his troopers, I figured the man was at best more administrator than soldier.

"Colonel Rattinger. I'm Jefferson Stottlemyre, United States Special Agent. I'm here by order of President Harrison to deal with whatever is killing your settlers or causing them to disappear." I wanted to let him know the federal government was still holding him responsible for the safety of the settlers living in his command area and that the government felt he had failed that duty, otherwise I wouldn't be in his office.

"Yes," he said. "I've just received a message from Secretary Elkins directing to me to give you whatever aid you desire, within reason." He frowned as he dropped the telegram. "I must tell you sir, I find this a damned inconvenience. I'm trying to close this post while still carrying out my duties to the people of this area." He stood up, and I could tell he was about to get into a full blown tirade. I decided to let him run with it. "For all we know, those missing settlers simply packed up and caught a train back to wherever they came from. There's been no indication of any activity from the local tribes now that we've stopped those damned drums. If there's something going on, it's a matter for the marshals, not the army, sir." He leaned across his desk and glared at me. "And I don't want to hear any blather about monsters. I've had crazies, white *and* red, trying to convince me there's some kind giant winged snake going around murdering people. I won't hear any more fairy tales, sir. I won't!"

"Then I won't tell you any. What I will tell you is that the cooperation I require is for you to add a night patrol around Crying Woman Mound. I need someone out there from dusk until dawn, Colonel."

"Impossible, sir. I simply don't have the manpower to spare. I cannot grant your request, no matter what Washington desires. You have no idea what it takes to maintain a cavalry troop in the field, Mr. Stottlemyre."

I crossed my arms, feeling my frown deepen. I could see why the War Department had left him here in the backwaters of nowhere to shut down an aging and redundant army post. "Colonel, before you start trying to tell me about cavalry, I want to ask you, have you ever heard of Grierson's Raid?"

He paused and blinked a few times. "Of course, Mr. Stottlemyre."

I wasn't surprised. If he hadn't heard of Grierson's Raid he wasn't a cavalry man, no matter the crossed sabers on his uniform. The raid was a fifteen hundred mile running attack by Colonel Benjamin Grierson's Union cavalry through the heart of the south, especially Mississippi. Rebel arms were captured, supply chains disrupted, train tracks and engines destroyed, and it was such a large disruption to southern logistics that it helped Grant get a strangle grip on Vicksburg.

"I was a captain under Colonel Grierson during that raid. I understand exactly what a troop of cavalry can and cannot do; I understand the missions they are equipped to undertake. With their home fort so close, what I am asking is simple enough. You can keep those men in the field for as long as the fort's supplies hold out or until you move the entire company to Camp Wichita." I leaned back and stared him down. "I can't force you to comply, of course, but I can remind you that you have orders."

We stared at each other for several minutes. Finally, back stiff, he marched to the door and pulled it open. The sergeant was standing outside, waiting to escort us back off the fort grounds, no doubt. He snapped to attention in the face of his angry colonel.

"Sergeant Perkins, select nine men to take with you on a night patrol. You'll be working the area around Crying Woman, over by Hennessey Corner. You can keep an eye out for those drumming savages while you're patrolling. Be prepared to receive full orders before evening mess. In the meantime, please escort these gentlemen off the grounds."

The sergeant snapped a salute. "Yes, sir," annoyance at pulling night patrol written all over his face. "Please follow me."

As far as I was concerned we were done here, and I wanted to take a little ride around Hennessey Corner before heading back to Binger. I wanted to make a plan, and after last night I wanted to rest my weary bones. I wasn't sure I was doing the right thing by putting such a weak patrol in danger from the snake-god, but I wanted armed backup in place if we needed to fight off the monster's minions, human or snake, or in case we needed to evacuate some of the local homesteads. The fort looked as good a place as any other to make a stand, if it all fell apart.

Outside of Hennessey Corner, we picked up our shadows again, ten men this time instead of three. More locals had joined the Tesch boys, it seemed, and decided to make a run at us. They turned their horses to cut us off from the cart road to Binger.

Kicking my horse, I pulled the rifle from the saddle boot and wished I had a nice normal Winchester. I didn't want to waste this special ammunition on a bunch of hot-headed locals when I had a real monster to fight. I made a promise to myself that I'd buy a rifle in Binger, if we made it back. I tried to flatten myself down as I guided my mustang into a small stand of trees, little more than a thicket and shrubs. I looked over my shoulder. Blenchy's horse was falling behind mine, and the riders where closing the distance on him. The closest rider fired at us, but the range was too far. He was just wasting bullets. I pulled back on the reins.

"Marshal Rich is with them," Blenchy shouted as he drew abreast of me. "Must be a posse."

That changed things, being pursued by the law. Rich must have decided to go ahead and make his arrest attempt, and I didn't want to get into a shootout with a posse. All kinds of sticky legal issues would crop up at that point, and Marshal Thomas would have to get involved, most likely. I had to wonder what the town of Hennessey Corner was trying to hide or protect. I was pretty sure it was connected to the creature in the hill, but I still didn't have any direct evidence.

"We could split up," Blenchy called. "You'd make it back to Binger for sure."

"I ain't explaining to Priscilla why I left you alone with a bunch of crazies chasing you. She'd have my damned throat torn out before I'd know what hit me. Now shut up and ride." The trees around us thickened, and we were forced to slow to a trot. My only consolation was that our pursuers would have to slow as well. I turned us back north, still trying to make our way to Binger while looking for a game trail to follow. Being in Binger would cut down on the trouble Rich could make for us.

The sounds of beating hooves and gunfire forced us to spur the horses to greater speed as a bullet struck the tree in front of me and sent bits of bark flying. The damned fools were running their horses in this mess. It was only matter of time before broken legs and broken riders followed.

Branches grabbed at us, slashed through clothes and against suddenly exposed skin. Blenchy's horse whinnied. I glanced over to see flared nostrils and eyes rolling in near panic and possibly pain. Blenchy was leaning over the saddle, blood spreading down his left arm as he clung to the saddle, desperate to hold onto the horse in the thick trees and down a steep slope.

The whole thing was a disaster waiting to happen. I had a good horse, cavalry training, and the better weapon. It was time to use them in a manner of my own choosing. "Keep running for Binger, Bill!" I shouted. "Don't stop. I'll catch up."

I pulled my horse up as Blenchy's horse found a game trail and darted away, despite his curses. I dropped the rifle back in the boot and drew my Schofield, leaning over the saddle just like on that wild nighttime ride through rebel territory. I turned the mustang and kicked him toward our pursuers, a one-man cavalry charge. Or cavalry trot. The branches snagged at my jacket and I lost my damned hat, but I broke right into the front of their formation, such as it was, firing at the surprised man riding point. He toppled from the saddle, and his horse turned hard right and cut off that side of the riders.

I turned into the other group, firing twice more as they scattered like panicked birds before me. I made for a clearing ahead, turning in the saddle and firing again while hoping my horse had more sense than I did and wouldn't trip or run into a tree. The pursuers milled around a bit, Marshal Rich returning fire.

I hoped Bill was away and safe. I holstered my gun and rode right back into the trees, pushing the horse recklessly as I did, until we broke from the stand of blackjacks and gum belly. I kicked him hard to put some distance between us and the tree line, and the little mustang responded like a champion, breaking into a gallop. I drew the rifle from the saddle boot and worked the bolt. Settling into the horse's rhythm, I twisted in the saddle as the lynch-mob-as-posse, missing more than a couple of riders, broke cover. I fired once before turning my focus to escape. There was a satisfying explosion followed by screams behind me.

It was enough to force them to break off, because the rest of the ride was uneventful, if a bit too chaotic and hell-bent for my personal taste. I met up with Blenchy on the outskirts of Binger. His shirt was bloody, and his horse seemed more winded than mine. He had his Colt in hand. "It's just a graze," Blenchy said. "The horse got hit worse."

I saw where the limping horse had taken a bullet in the flank. It was a wonder the animal was still moving at all. I got off my mustang and made Bill get on. Graze or no, he'd lost some blood, and his horse might collapse at any minute. I walked the last half-mile or so, filling Blenchy in as we traveled.

We made our way back to Binger without anyone else trying to kill us, passing a couple of draft wagons full of baled cotton and a handful of other riders about their business. We unloaded and paid the stable hand extra to have the horse taken care of, though if anyone in town could dig a bullet out of the animal, I'd be surprised. I tried to talk Blenchy into heading over to the doctor's office, but he insisted that it was only a graze and that Priscilla or Violet could just as easily pour a little whiskey over it and bandage him right up, though he worried that this was the second shirt he'd destroyed in as many days and what would Priscilla say.

Walking back to the hotel, we found the whole town abuzz with anger, and that was when I noticed all the dead snakes piled up near one of the saloons. The townsfolk turned to look at us, but after noticing the badges, the blood, and the no-nonsense way we moved, they turned back to the stack of serpents. We fell under the angry glare of Hank Tesch, who was no longer preaching but instead was standing on the porch of the Klingman's Dry Goods, leaning against a rail. I knew the Tesch boys were going to keep right on being trouble for us, and I wished they'd just go ahead and make their play.

Lady Priscilla and Violet were waiting for us in the hotel lobby, Lady Priscilla looking pale and drawn, Violet ready to chew barbed wire and buzzing with energy.

SIX

I watched William and Marshal Stottlemyre ride down
the road toward the cursed town of Hennessey Corner, where
they planned to scout the monster's lair at Crying Woman
Mound before riding on to Fort Cobb to seek aid from the
local Army detachment. Red dust kicked up under the hoofs
of their horses as they turned around a bend heading up from
the gentle valley made by the stream the locals called Sugar
Creek. As they vanished from sight, I turned from the
window of the hotel to find Violeta watching me with
concern.

Last night had been too close, too close in more ways
than my love and companions would ever know. So close
that I would never tell them, though I suspected Violeta had
an idea. William might as well, no matter the distraction of
last night's love-making.

There had been a moment, as I undressed and changed
into the wolf, when I felt it, a pull so strong that it took all the
control I held over the wolf to not tear howling into the
night, searching for prey, searching for a kill. I had been too
much the wolf these past few days. Though I could control
my changes, that control was razor thin, and the true full
moon would be in the sky tonight. I was tired. So very tired
of fighting the change. My body was weary from
transforming from human to wolf and from expelling the
venom from my system. Tonight it would be so easy to give
myself over, to run and run forever.

To run from William.

To give him the freedom he deserved, the freedom to
find a love who could provide him the family I could not. My
body would never allow me to bear a child. The change
would destroy any babe in my womb. The drugs to keep me
human were poison to any not suffering my affliction, so no

miracle would allow me to give my mate the children he wanted. I loved him but feared I should not.

"We should go, mistress."

I turned to dear Violeta. She had become a rock to which I could cling when troubled by the dark thoughts that filled my mind, thoughts I sometimes found myself loath to share with William. She picked up William's ruined shirt from last night and tossed it into the little room she was sleeping in, no doubt to cut the linen down for bandages. We seemed to need a steady supply of them. I wondered not for the first time how long it would be before this life killed William or me. Or Violeta. I knew I would be unable to stand losing Violeta as I had poor Nettie, and if I were to lose William…

"Yes," I said. "Yes. Let us see if Mr. Brinkerhoff is available."

We finished dressing, Violeta hiding various weapons about my person and in my bag. In a village full of innocent citizens, I would be unable and unwilling to become the wolf should danger present itself. Even were we in the field, the wolf was an option of last resort for the next few days. I tucked the letter of introduction and inquiry Marshal Stottlemyre had written for me to Mr. Brinkerhoff into my sleeve as Violeta armed herself, openly carrying one of her revolvers and a long knife, almost a short side sword. I had no doubt she had concealed other items in her clothing. Satisfied, she opened the door and followed me out of the suite.

We inquired as to the location of the local photography studio and were directed to the home of Mr. Charles A. Olson, whose studio was built into the back of his dwelling. I thanked the gentleman behind the counter despite his obvious discomfort with Violeta, and we set off into the cool morning.

The first screams reached my ears well before we reached Mr. Olson's home. Violeta immediately placed herself between me and the unseen danger. There followed the sounds of weapons firing, running, and more screaming.

A moment later a group of terrified men, women, and children raced toward us, pursued by a horde of snakes.

I froze in place, images of last night's frantic battle clouding my mind. Coldness crept into my chest as perspiration ran in streams down my unresponsive body. The lead snakes lashed out, striking a boy no older than ten, who stumbled and collapsed onto the dirt street. As the poor boy pitched down face first, the fear that had held me broke, replaced by anger. I rushed toward the fallen child. Violeta leapt forward, revolver drawn and long knife flashing, carving a path through the serpents. They broke around us and scattered as several men with harvesting tools, clubs, and other weapons charged to join us. Sporadic gunfire let us know the battle was going on in other parts of town. I looked up the street at a familiar form leaning against a building. Marshal Widner had been bitten, it seemed. Three men lifted him and jogged away toward one of the main street taverns.

Violeta cursed and pointed. "They come from that house."

The door to the white-washed, wood-framed building was open, and as we watched, a dozen or more snakes exited through the door and across the porch, making their way into the town. It was the photographer's home. Gathering my skirts and drawing the small revolver from my bag, I ran behind Violeta, who cleared the stoop of our slithering opponents and continued her charge inside.

We found him slumped against at the end of the long hall. He was an older man, well into his sixth decade. His breaths were coming raspy, and it was if I could see the venom rushing through him, bringing him to his investable death. "Edith?" he whispered.

I knelt next to him. "No, sir. I—I was coming to see Mr. Brinkerhoff. I—I shall summon you a doctor right away."

He grasped my arm as I tried to move away, his rheumy blue eyes straining to focus. "Went to Crying Woman. He and that Halfmoon boy. He found…in his pictures…the door… the iron door…and other…things. In the pictures…lizard folk…said it must be a malfunction….oh, my Edith…" His voice faded, as did the light in his eyes. They closed forever and he slumped, limp.

"Mistress, we must go!" Violeta, covered in snake gore, long knife dripping, stood with her back to me, facing the hallways and stairs.

"We have to find the photographs." The hotel clerk had told us Mr. Olson's studio was in the back of the house, and we appeared to be at the end of the hallway. Standing, I twisted the doorknob and pushed the door inward. Olson's dead body fell onto its back. Grimly, I stepped over him into the workroom.

The man's camera was in one corner, a large, black, box-like affair. A cabinet with various odd and ends I couldn't identify stood with its double doors open. There were two high-backed chairs and a settee, and a variety of drapes and tiebacks. The black drop cloth used to hide mothers in the portraits of their children lay folded on a side table. A small white wood coffin, child-sized, was propped in a corner. There was door that I suspected led to the darkroom. Tossed on the work table were a handful of prints, one of which I recognized even from this distance as Brinkerhoff's picture of the cavalry.

I walked over to it as Violeta, watching nervously, moved to block the door, standing over poor Mr. Olson's body. There was a door in the photograph on the hill behind the cavalry troop lines up and mounted, posing for the camera. Why none of us had been able to see it, I didn't understand, but I recalled the conversation between Mrs. Creswell and the other lady about hidden Spanish gold. I shook my head, amazed at the magic it must take to hide the door from our sight. I shuffled through the next few prints until I came to one Mr. Brinkerhoff must had have taken of the mob outside the McHenry farm through a window. In the foreground was the side of William's horse. I recognized his trousers and boots. The mob faced them from the yard.

They were not all human.

A handful of the citizens of Hennessey Corner, mostly those at the back of the mob, appeared to have quite reptilian features, including nostril slits on slightly elongated snouts and eyes like those on the snakes that had attacked us. A few even seemed to have scales gleaming in the light. The most disturbing was in the back, riding a black horse toward the group. I recognized the rider from her clothes, but otherwise she was only human in build and shape. Beside her rode Marshal Rich. Lizard people. Truly. Mrs. Creswell was a humanoid lizard, as were other villagers. Well.

I gathered the photographs. If these were to fall into the wrong hands, the iron door might start a run of treasure seekers to the mound, which I feared would prove fatal to the adventurers. The photographic evidence of serpent people, blurry as it might be, might cause a panic. Violeta and I checked the rest of the house for survivors and found the body of an older woman we supposed must have been the Edith poor departed Mr. Olson kept calling for.

We exited the house to find a panic underway. The citizens of Binger were now looking for both an explanation and a place to lay blame, and with Marshal Widner incapacitated or possibly even dead, there was no one to calm the crowd.

"It's those folks over in Hennessey Corner," one voice called out. "They've always been a strange bunch. I hear that old Granny Creswell is a witch, bound to Old Scratch himself. She's been turning the other women in town away from godliness, teaching them incantations and all that."

"It's the cavalry! They stopped the drumming."

"Maybe the cavalry didn't really stop the drums. Maybe the Injuns stopped a-purpose to set this snake plague on us."

"I don't believe in any of this magic crock, but them Caddo families have been angry since the government opened up the territory. I think they caught all these snakes and set 'em on us, trying to scare us away."

"The Kepping woman, she keeps herself close around Creswell's house. Old Mr. Pent's cow went dry, and his hens stopped laying after he argued with Sarah Kepping about her pig rooting under his fence."

The crowd seemed primed to exploded, and I did not want Violeta and myself, as visitors and outsiders, to become targets of the villagers' frustrations and fears. We moved as quickly as possible away from the people yelling in front of the pub and retreated toward the hoped-for safety of the hotel. The lobby was empty when we returned, and I suspected the desk clerk had joined the rest of the villagers outside. Violeta and I walked up the steps, and as I walked into the room my mind was so focused on the photographs that I didn't notice that the door was unlocked, nor did the strange scents register as danger.

I'm unsure who was more surprised, I or the two men tossing about my and William's possessions. I recognized the street-preaching Tesch brother. The other man was similar to the first in height and appearance, though he looked a bit younger. His left arm as held in a sling.

They turned as I entered, the older looking up from where he was rummaging through William's bag and muttering, "Damn."

The younger one, his face turning hard, shook off his surprise and started toward me, his uninjured hand outstretched as if to grab my by the front of my blouse and drag me the rest of the way into the room. I stepped into the room of my own free will, moving sideways as I did. The older brother reached for his gun at the same time I heard Violeta work the hammer on her own weapon.

"Stop." My voice was low and harsh. The younger man froze in place. "Stop right now before someone gets hurt." The older brother yanked at the younger one's collar as Violeta entered the room, revolver unwavering as she menaced the two men. "I would thank you two gentlemen to leave my rooms before I summon the marshal."

"Marshal Widner ain't gonna be helping no one no more, I'm thinking," said the older man, regaining some bravado. "Saw 'em carrying him to where Doc Meaghan was tending the injured at Lewises' place. Reckon he might not even survive that snakebite."

"No matter. I could simply order my maid to shot you. Breaking into a woman's hotel room and threatening her, I wonder how the nice villagers of Binger would react? I suspect you would find yourself in dire—"

The older man pushed his brother right at Violeta, the startled young man leaving his feet for an instant before he landed and stumbled into her. She fired once, but the man's body cut her off at the knees, and she fell. The older one was right behind, charging in the same way I had seen William do in the past. He struck with his fist before I could move entirely out of his way, catching me not in the face, but on my shoulder. I spun away, dropping the photographs on the floor.

There was grunt and a scramble, and I caught a glimpse of the younger man on the floor. His eyes opened wide at one of the pictures before he snatched it up in his good hand with an exclamation of, "The door! They found it!"

Whatever the older Tesch was going to say was cut off as Violeta rose to one knee and lifted her revolver. He had the sense to throw himself out the door in a graceless plunge to safety, and I heard him scrambling on the hallway floor before he rolled down the stairs. The younger man lunged at Violeta, knocking her flat. He followed his brother before I could stop him. Violeta, cursing in Bulgarian, gathered herself and stood, pistol in hand.

"No," I told her. "No, let us arm ourselves and wait for William and Marshal Stottlemyre."

Violeta reloaded, still cursing under her breath. I gathered up Brinkerhoff's photographs, realizing the young man had taken the one of the iron door in the side of the mound. A part of me wanted to chase after them. We had no idea how long William and Marshal Stottlemyre would be out. Brinkerhoff and Halfmoon would be in terrible danger, but the entire encounter had left me shaken, and my shoulder hurt from where Hank Tesch had punched me. I wanted food, water, and rest. Armed and wary, still clutching the remaining photographs, we retired to the hotel restaurant for refreshment, watching the street for signs of William, the Tesch brothers, or new trouble about to descend upon us.

SEVEN

I sat on the wooden stool as Priscilla cleaned my arm where the bullet had grazed me, wiping away the dried blood and going at the wound with alcohol to prevent infection. All of us had become adept field medics.

"This was one of your better shirts," she said in disgust.

"Sorry."

"Well, now you only have one decent shirt left, so you'd best take care of it."

"Yes, dear."

"Don't you 'yes, dear' me. Someday you are going to have a wound that goes gangrene and then what? I'll tell you what. I will be forced to bite off a finger or hand or God forbid part of your arm, and then where will we be, hmm?"

Keeping my mouth shut seemed to smartest course of action, so I did. The only reason I hadn't turned right back around and started hunting Hank Tesch was because Priscilla insisted she was uninjured, but she moved stiffly as she wrapped my arm in a bandage to keep dirt from getting into the wound. I felt lucky she didn't have to go digging a piece of clothing out of my wound. Again.

Jefferson came back into the room as I was putting on my last shirt, Violet trailing behind, a silent shadow carrying an infantry rifle on her shoulder. She had insisted that Jefferson have someone watching his back, and once Violet started insisting it seemed smarter to let her have her head. She moved to the window, standing off to the side and peering out, watching for trouble.

"Well?" I asked.

"I think I've got them settled down." Jefferson sat down on the edge of the bed. "I deputized a couple of the steadier one. That should keep them out of trouble until Widner's ready to take 'em in hand."

"Will the marshal survive?" Priscilla asked.

"Yeah. Doc Meaghan said most of the folks will live."

"Most?" Priscilla held herself very still.

"Five are dead so far, including that photographer and his wife." Jefferson took off his hat and scratched his head. "I promised I'd send the cavalry over to help protect the town."

"Is that likely?" I asked.

"Sent a telegram over to the fort explaining the town was attacked. Didn't bother to say by who." He took a deep breath, and I could feel the weariness in him from across the room. "I'd like to stay and keep things under control here, but I need to get out there and find Brinkerhoff and Halfmoon."

"And there's the Tesch boys to deal with," I added. I had business with Hank Tesch. No one strikes my lady and just walks away. No one.

"I reckon we'll be dealing with them soon enough. I saw the three of them talking together near the Post Office. I figure they'll try to stop us from getting to Crying Woman. I really figure they're going to come after Lady Priscilla—"

Priscilla huffed in frustration. "Please, Jefferson, we've been so through so much together. I am simply Priscilla, and you can address me by my name."

"Yes, ma'am. I figure they're going to come after Priscilla and Violet. They've seen the photograph and know how to find the door."

"Well, we can't go haring off after that damned Brinkerhoff and leave Priscilla here and…" I paused and looked at my love. She had an eyebrow raised. "You need to stay out of your wolf-skin for as long as you can, and I hate the idea of leaving you and Violet here. I know you can both take damned good care of yourselves, but we know them Tesch boys will be coming after you, since you had that photograph."

"You don't know for sure that they'll attack." Priscilla said, the frown on her face telling me she didn't believe what she had just said any more than I did.

69

"They will attack," Violet said softly. She was peering out the window, standing off to the side so she had cover. "They are coming. Two of them."

Jefferson was at the window before I could move, and since there was no sense all of us crowding around, I decided to give my weapons a quick check. "Well?" I asked.

"The preaching one is heading toward the hotel. The one who chased us with the Hennessey mob just broke off and started around behind the dry goods store. I can't see the third boy anywhere—"

The crack of the rifle and Violet's scream were almost instantaneous. Violet crashed backward onto the bed, red blood spraying around her. The bullet passed through her and smashed the oval mirror over the chest of drawers, sending sharp shards flying. Jefferson dived away from the window, and I had to pull Priscilla down to the floor before she made a target of herself trying to reach Violet. Violet rolled off the bed and landed hard on the floor with a cry of pain as the second shoot shook the bed, the bullet hitting one of the goose-feather pillows where Violet had been seconds before.

"Damn it," Jefferson muttered. "I can't see where he is."

"That sounds like a Spencer." I'd used the repeating rifle and knew what it could do. "Even if we can't see him, I think we know where that third Tesch boy is."

"You reckon they brought any help?"

"No. They would want the gold for themselves," Priscilla said from the floor. She was using a corner of the quilt to try and staunch the flow of blood from Violet's shoulder. Violet was shaking, her eyes wide in pain and shock. "I'm going to get the medical bag." Keeping low to the floor, Priscilla made her way toward the little side room Violet had been sleeping in.

I studied the angle of the shots. If I could get at the window without getting my fool head shot off, I could probably figure out where the Tesch boy was shooting from. I crept along the floor, over Violet's legs and through her blood, until I was under the window. Carefully, I snatched up

70

the other pillow and held it at the window. It flew from my hand at the impact of the bullet, and I poked my head up for an instant, giving the area a quick survey. "He's either on the water tower at the rail yard or in the church belfry," I said, ducking. "I'm betting on the church. It's closer and has better cover. He ain't using a Sharps, so the water tower would be a stretch."

Priscilla crawled back into the room, dragging a bag in her right hand. She settled next to Violet, who had stopped shaking and closed her eyes, muttering in Bulgarian. "Don't you dare die on me, Violeta Tsankova," Priscilla muttered. I glanced down at Violet. Her wound was ugly, covering her blouse in blood. It was good that the bullet had passed through her shoulder, but she was in danger of bleeding to death if Priscilla couldn't halt the flow.

"You're going to have to stitch her up," I said softly.

"She needs a doctor's hand, not mine," Priscilla hissed.

"Darling, I can't promise you when we'll be able to get the doc over here to help."

"Give us ten minutes," Jefferson said. We both looked up at him. "Bill, I need you to get to another room, even the roof. Deal with that Tesch boy out there trying to pick us off. I'll handle Hank and his brother."

"I'm not sure about leaving Priscilla and Violet..."

Violet opened her eyes and raised her revolver, pointing it at the door and setting it on her lap. "I will watch."

"And when you pass out?" I demanded.

"Then I'll hear them approach and deal with them accordingly," Priscilla said softly. She glared up at me. "You're the only one who can stop the sharpshooter. Marshal Stottlemyre is experienced in handling pistol engagements. I'm very good at close-range killing." She drew her own revolver, a little Webley Bulldog, from her purse. "Hearing and reflexes of a wolf."

"Priscilla..."

"Go, love. We'll be fine."

I looked over at Jefferson. He added a sixth round in his Schofield and snapped it closed. "Ready, Bill? You could take Tesla's fancy rifle."

"No," I told him. "My old one will do fine." I moved away from the window. Keeping low, I slipped around to the chest and drew out a box of cartridges for my rifle. I crawled on my hands and knees until I was sure I was out of any likely line of sight and hefted my old rifle. I gave Priscilla a long look where she knelt tending Violet. She smiled at me. I nodded and stepped out the door, Jefferson right behind me. There was a scream and gunfire from the lobby.

"Time to earn my money," Jefferson said.

"I'm not sure you're getting paid." He gave me a sour look. "I'm just telling you, I don't remember Marshal Thomas saying anything about pay when he handed you that badge."

"Well then, maybe I've been working too hard." He smiled at me as Hank Tesch's voice yelled down in the lobby for everyone to get out. "See you in a few minutes." He started down the stairs, Schofield in hand. "Hell, the idiot's already wasted one into the damned ceiling."

I jogged down to the end of the hallway, stopping at the last room. I reach out and tried the door. It was unlocked. Stepping inside, I carefully eased over to the window. I could see both the water tower and the church bells from here. I'd be shooting upward. About seventy-five yards to the church and maybe two hundred to the water tower; longs shots for a Spencer or Winchester in the hands of an expert, dead easy for my Sharps.

The trick was getting the kid to reveal himself. I would have to wait for him to make a mistake. I knelt next to the window on the floor, opened the breech, and selected a regular lead round. No senses wasting good silver on another man. Slowly easing forwards, rifle aimed at the church where I thought the youngest Tesch might be, I rested the barrel on the windowsill while trying to keep it from being obvious and watching the dark shadows near the bell. Resting my cheek where my Granny Coulton had carved one of her hex symbols—the same kind she drew on barns—I felt the warmth of the rifle's magic fill me. The Sharps, my father's rifle and his gift to me as he lay dying from a fever caused by a federal soldier's bullet, had never missed when I needed— *truly needed*—to hit a target. Over the years I had added my own blood and magic to the hex mark, just as my granny had taught me, keeping the charm fresh. As I felt it settle about me, I knew in my soul and bones how important it was for us to deal with the Tesch boys and get to Crying Woman. The weight of existence and possibly the fate of all I knew rested on my next shot.

I glanced past the church to the water tower from time to time, keeping in mind the possibility the young man might be lurking there. I heard a door slam shut somewhere in the hotel, followed by a short exchange of gunfire, all of it muffled by the walls and floors. It took all my willpower to resist the urge to check behind me or call out to my comrades. I adjusted the sights on the Sharps and waited, recited Shakespeare's 71st sonnet in my head because it helped soothe me. Another shot from downstairs, followed by two in quick succession. Breathe in. Breathe out. Watch. Wait. Breathe.

It wasn't much, almost too little for a man to die over. I caught the barest glint of the lowering sun off the barrel of a rifle in the church belfry. Young Tesch had probably shifted his position, trying for a better angle or wanting to get a bead on a target. I drew a long breath as he fired, the muzzle flash dimmed by daylight but still visible. I lined up my own shot, set the rear trigger, took up the slack, and exhaled, giving the front trigger a gentle squeeze, the barest kiss of a butterfly's wings on a soft cheek. The Sharps roared and kicked into my shoulder, familiar and comforting as the magic broke around me and the bullet speed on its inevitable course.

The barrel of Tesch's Spencer lifted upward and fell back as something heavy hit the bell and set it ringing. I watched the spot for a handful of minutes. I hadn't *seen* if I'd killed my opponent or not. He could be dead on the floor of the bell tower, but I couldn't see him, and I refused to assume.

Counting off two full minutes in my head, I started to relax when there was no sign of the Tesch boy surviving. I hated killing. Men or animals, I hated it. I'd killed, of course. Men, monsters, men who were monsters, but that boy was just a youngster who'd followed his older brothers down the wrong path. Death by poor life choices. It didn't seem fair.

I opened the breech of the rifle and reached for another cartridge, had it halfway in when I head the barest scuff of a boot on the wooden floor. I rolled sideways, using the bed for cover as the pop of the gun and smash of the bullet into the wooden window frame happened in an instant. I pushed the cartridge into the breech, closed it, and cocked back the hammer, looking at my would-be ambusher's feet from my prone position on the far side of the bed. He took two quick steps toward me and leapt onto the bed, the whole thing sagging and groaning. I rolled onto my back and tried to bring my long gun to bear as the second Tesch brother loomed over me, Colt at point-blank.

Two quick, loud shots rang out in the little room, and Tesch jerked twice, his eyes going wide. He blinked and started to turn around, the pistol in his hand lowering as if it had suddenly become too heavy for him to carry. A third and fourth shot and the room filled with powder smoke. Tesch collapsed to his knees. "Hell," he murmured and pitched over face-first onto the bed. He took two breaths, the last exhale a soft, rattling wheeze before his body went limp.

I rose up from the floor and peered over the corpse. Priscilla stood in the doorway, her little English revolver in her right hand, smoke still curling from the end of the barrel. "All right, my love?" she asked.

I stood and walked around the bed, ignoring the dead man. "Thanks for watching my back." I decided I needed to kiss her right then and there, so I did. The kiss was long and hard, and when I finally pulled back, I could see the wolf in her smile, in the flare of her nostrils and the flush of her cheeks. "I am right pleased to see you."

"And I am delighted to find you alive. Have you dealt with the sharpshooter?"

"He ain't shooting at us."

"Very good." She kissed me again and growled softly. "We should assist Jefferson." She stepped back and through the door into the hallway.

"You got any extra rounds for your little toy?"

"My little toy saved your life."

"I had it under control."

"Of course you did, dear." She opened the black purse dangling off her wrist and began reloading her little revolver. We passed our room, door closed, and I hoped Violet was safe and alive. Priscilla snapped the chamber shut as we reached the top of the stairs and looked at me, a playful smile on her lips.

I grinned back at her. There was no one else I wanted at my side if it was going to come to a fight with Hank Tesch. I made sure my Colt was sitting easy in its holster, lowered the barrel of the Sharps level, and started down the stairs.

Drawing my little Colt .31 from my boot and dropping it into my trouser pocket, I started down the stairs toward the hotel lobby, Schofield in hand, determined to deal with Hank Tesch. My hope was that all the civilians in the lobby had fled or taken cover, because although I had my badge pinned onto my vest, I doubted Hank was the kind of man who cared about a bit of silver. All the authority he likely understood was through strength and violence. Still, I'd try to talk him down, make him see sense. Assuming he didn't just start shooting at me right off. I could have wished the hotel had a way to the lobby besides the central staircase, but if wishes were horses…

Easing around the final turn of the stairway, I peered through the bannister rail down into the lobby. Hank held a revolver in his right hand and was standing at the sign-in counter, menacing the desk clerk. I couldn't see or hear anyone else. It would have been easy enough to shoot Tesch down from here, but it didn't sit right, shooting him in the back.

Warranted or not, I knew I had a reputation as a dangerous gunman, mostly based on a handful of shootouts with thieves and robbers during my time as a marshal in the Dakota Territories. Maybe the reputation would be good for something. Hank was busy waving his pistol at the frightened clerk, demanding that the man leave, so I finished coming down the stairs until I was almost at the bottom. I could dive off to the side and get behind a tall chair in an instant. I raised my pistol.

"Hank Tesch," I said softly, "you need to put that gun away."

He turned toward me, surprise writ large on his face. His eyes gave a quick search of the room, as if looking for something, probably his brother.

I held my gun steady. "I know you and your brother attacked a couple of ladies today. If you stop this now, it won't go so hard on you."

"That gold's ours," he finally said. "We've been hunting for it. You ain't taking it."

"There's no gold in that hill, son. Just death."

He looked at my unwavering gun. For a moment, I thought he might back down, thought he might use some sense and drop his weapon or flee out the front door. I'd have been happy for either result. Instead, a door slammed somewhere behind me, and I realized there must be stairs or a ladder on the far side of the building to escape from a fire. The third Tesch boy had gotten into the building and was behind me somewhere. That's what Hank was waiting on.

I moved to my left for the cover of the chair as Hank brought up his pistol to bear. He fired twice in quick succession, one bullet smashing into the wood bannister and sending splinters flying. I fired once in return, slow and deliberate, and watched the blood blossom on the left shoulder of his shirt. We exchanged another shot each as he staggered back. I felt something burn across my arm as a second splotch of red materialized in the middle of Hank's shirt. There was a pause as he stumbled back against the counter. I kept moving, drawing my smaller pistol, ready for the other Tesch to appear even as I engaged Hank.

I shot Hank again as he cocked back the hammer of his Colt. He slumped against the counter and fell down, his own shot going into the floor. He worked his hammer again and pulled the trigger, the barrel still aimed at the floor. It fell on an empty. I chanced a glance over my shoulder, seeking anyone coming up behind me. The sound of a gun cocking made me look back. Hank had drawn a double barreled derringer from a pocket. He lifted the little pistol and started to aim it at me.

I shot him in the middle of the chest. He jerked back from the impact, dropped the derringer, and slumped over, eyes closed, body limp. I stood over him for a moment and shifted my weight, turning my head to check for ambush. The front window shattered as I felt another burn across my neck, followed by the roar of Blenchy's rifle and the church bells ringing. I dived to the floor to present less of a target and started to crawl for cover behind the counter. I rolled into a sitting position, nodded to the wide-eyed clerk, who was clutching a shotgun, and snapped opened my Schofield, quickly exchanging the empty cartridges for live rounds. Two small pops followed by two more echoed down the stairs, and I hoped Blenchy hadn't been ambushed by the last of the Tesch brothers. I slipped around the counter and dashed to the stairs as the church bells faded and stilled, both pistols drawn.

At the landing, I found a smiling Bill Blenchy and Priscilla Talbot. Priscilla's smile dropped, and before I was sure what had happened, I was in their room, pressing a clean cloth to the graze on my neck as Pricilla treated the shallow wound across the top of my shoulder. We were an injured and bedraggled lot, and there was still too much to do and too many places we needed to be at once. The wounds Blenchy and I had suffered over the last day wouldn't kill us if they didn't get infected. Violet was in worse shape, but we got Doc Meaghan to come and look her over. With the bullet passing through her shoulder, all he could do was finish stitching her up and setting her arm in a sling. She had orders to rest in bed. I could by looking in her eyes she would disobey those orders the moment she thought Priscilla was in danger.

The Tesch boys had been dealt with and their bodies carted off to the undertaker, but we still needed to get to Crying Woman. Brinkerhoff and Halfmoon were walking into a danger none of us were ready to face. Priscila made us stop and eat, which took longer than I expected since we had to coax the hotel staff back to work after Hank's rampage. After too long a time, we were all seated downstairs eating dinner, even Violet, who had insisted she could manage the stairs.

"I think Jefferson and I should go. Just the two of us," Blenchy finally said. His eyes were steady as he watched for Priscilla's reaction. "Someone needs to stay here and be ready to deal with any things that get past us or decided to attack the town."

"And why should that be me? Why would anyone listen to me if we're attacked?" Priscilla's voice was terse, but she didn't dismiss the notion out-of-hand. "I admit the assistance and reaction of the locals to our battle with the Tesch brothers was slow."

"Nonexistent," I muttered. So much for the folks I'd tried to deputize. They'd mostly stayed away from the gun battle. I guess I couldn't really blame them; they were good solid folks, but they were all spooked. My biggest worry was that fear would make them an unruly mob.

"You're right," Blenchy said. "They likely won't listen to you, being a woman and a foreigner to boot, but they'll listen to Marshal Thomas." Blenchy pointed out the shattered window. Marshal Henry Thomas was riding down the street, flanked by another man. "If you come with us to Crying Woman, the chances are good you'll need to change skin," he whispered. "If you stay here you might not need to, but you can if the threat is enough." He set his fork down. "I'd rather you didn't change for the next couple of days, unless it's an emergency. The full moon is tonight, and you've been in your other form a lot lately."

Her lips thinned, but she nodded her head. "Agreed. I don't want to leave the villagers undefended, should the monster attack here."

"Then it's settled. We'll tell Marshal Thomas what's going on, and then Bill and I will head to Crying Woman."

It took us a half an hour to tell Marshal Thomas the whole tale. He offered to send his deputy—a quiet, tall black man named Bass Reeves—along with us, but we declined once Thomas told me that every local member of the Caddo and Wichita tribes were heading to Binger and hoped for sanctuary. I knew he'd need all the help he could get keeping the peace right here.

It was near dusk when Blenchy and I set out from the town. The cavalry hadn't arrived from Fort Cobb despite my telegram, and I made a note to report Colonel Rattinger to the War Department if I survived.

As we rounded the little bend and started up out of the creek valley, we heard the faint sounds of drums in the distance. I nudged my horse to a trot and checked my Tesla Rifle. I didn't have a plan yet for stopping the monster beyond shooting it, and I wasn't sure that would even work. I glanced over at Bill Blenchy's serene face and prayed I wasn't leading us both to our deaths—or something worse.

EIGHT

It was hard watching my William ride away yet again, but I knew he was right: there was no time for me to play the waiting, wailing damsel whose lover had gone off to war and possible death. William and Marshal Stottlemyre needed to find the photographer and Mr. Halfmoon, and the beast in me sensed the matter would come to a head and play out to the end tonight. Marshal Stottlemyre held the weapon I knew would be effective against the Snake-God, and since we were missing Mr. Bloom or any other skilled sorcerer, William knew the most about magic among us. I had no idea if his knowledge and skills would be helpful tonight, but I felt better knowing the two men had ridden out together, though I could have wished they had a company of soldiers with them.

A company of soldiers, or at least a patrol, was what we had to defend Binger, should another attack on the village come. The proud young captain had ridden in followed by twenty-five of his men. There had been several tense moments as a mob of local villagers, the blue-uniformed soldiers, and a crowd of native refugees all converged near the rail station, everyone armed and on edge. The young army captain was determined to interrogate the natives about the drumming while deflecting the locals' angry questions. The villagers demanded to know why the army had not protected the village while accusing the natives of causing the attack. The natives were angry that the army had stopped their sacred drumming ritual and brought down ruin on them all, pleading that the greatest safety now lay in numbers. That the cleanup from the snake attack had only just finished and the drumming around the country side had grown louder and more instant did nothing to ease tensions.

Marshal Thomas and his deputy kept trying to mediate between the three groups, but the threat of a full-scale melee simmered and boiled. William and Marshal Stottlemyre had charged me with defending the village should it be attacked again by any supernatural agents, and I needed these three groups to work together in the face of such an attack. It was time to, as I once heard William express, grab the bull by the horns.

"Excuse me, gentlemen," I said softly, inserting myself into the middle of the argument. "I would speak with the captain, Marshal Thomas, whoever heads the village, and an appointed spokesman for the natives."

"Ma'am—"

"Miss—"

"I don' see how this is any—"

"Who do you think—...?"

"Now, gentlemen!" I brought the wolf forward, all the way to just before the change. My hair grew longer and thickened, my eyes changed from their usual brown to the predator's brown with yellow-tinting. One of my hands started to morph into a paw with long dark nails and canines grew in my mouth. "Now. Please. There are things coming, things beyond any terror you've imagined," I growled, allowing the change to fall away, though I knew if I started to change again, there would be no containing the beast inside of me.

"Dear Lord on high."

"I say."

"Monster—"

"*Tay-Sha*—"

"Wolf, actually," I said. "And at this this moment your best defense should the Snake-God of the mound come crashing down upon you."

"Now see here!" One of the villagers, a portly gentleman who was rapidly turning red, stepped up to me. "I don't know who you are, but we don't need any more deviltry in this town, and we sure don't need to be preached at by some twofer from the wrong side of the river!" There were murmurs from behind him, and I thought perhaps I'd been a bit rash.

Marshal Reeves drew his revolver and pointed it toward the sky as Marshal Thomas shouted, "Quiet! All of you. We all know something unnatural is happening here."

"It's them folk over in Hennessey Corner!" a woman's voice called out.

"Maybe so," Marshal Thomas agreed. "And President Harrison sent this woman and her companions here at the request of Governor Steele to help us deal with the devil in our midst. We're all scared, we're all tired, and we don't know what we're facing. But we need to stop standing around and yelling at each other and get to setting ourselves for a fight." He turned on the young army captain. "I expect you'd know best how to use your men, sir, so I'll leave you to it."

The captain nodded. "Sergeant, get the men mounted. Make sure they check their weapons. Establish a patrol around the town, fastest horses and riders. If something tries to attack, we need to be in position to intercept them."

An older man among the local natives stepped forward, a man perhaps the same age as Marshal Stottlemyre. He wore a faded blue uniform and carried a rifle with brass fittings. "If the Captain will accept my help, I'm a Adam Halfmoon. I was an officer in the army during the great war."

"I've meet your son, Lieutenant Halfmoon." The captain paused and nodded. "Very well, find any veterans who are willing to act as infantry or rifles and deploy them on the approaches to town. My own men are best used as a mobile force."

Marshal Thomas nodded his approval. "The rest of you folks, get your weapons and head to the center of town. We'll hole up in the salons, hotel, and jail. That ought to give us good line of sight from the windows. Put anyone who can't fight in the big church, and we'll post six good men to defend it." He turned to Adam Halfmoon. "The goes for your people as well. We need to be ready if they come—whatever they might be."

The sound of a rifle firing made everyone turn. Violeta stood in the middle of the red-dirt street, rifle in her hands, wobbling on weak legs as the sun started to dip below the horizon. Marshal Reeves rushed over to steady her, catching her before she collapsed. "They are coming," she called to the assemblage. "The serpent-people are coming, and they carry snakes. Many, many snakes."

NINE

Crying Woman loomed before us as the drumbeats echoed off the buttes and down the plains. It was too dark even with the full moon to follow any tracks Brinkerhoff and Halfmoon might have left, but I knew where the door would be from Priscilla's description. If the men we followed had gotten the door open somehow, then it would be obvious enough. If they hadn't, I reckoned we could get them to come back to Binger with us. Or we could drag them back.

The sounds of drumming grew louder and more intense, seeming to come from every direction at once, though we had seen no drummers. I checked behind us again. The Tesch boys might be resting in boxes, but Marshal Rich was still out there, as well as any number of possible lizard-folk. As for what Jefferson and I were riding to face...

Neither of us had spoken of it, but the air seemed charged with expectation, as if we were on the eve of a battle, a battle that would make the shootout with the Tesch brothers seem like an easy skirmish. Around us, the night had gone very still indeed. No sounds of animals great or small, not even a prairie breeze to stir the trees and tall grasses. My Sharps rested across my saddle in my hands, ready to be raised and fired with an instant's notice. Jefferson held the Tesla rifle in the same position, both of us half expecting the giant winged snake thing to descend on us at any moment.

It was hard to stay focused on the task at hand while part of my mind was back in Binger, worried about what Priscilla might have to face. Marshal Thomas and his deputy were likely enough to stand firm against the kind of dangers Priscilla and I had taken up facing for a living, but I suspected the townsfolk, already frightened and pushed to the brink of hysteria by the snake attack, might well buckle and fold their cards in the face of the horror stalking the countryside. I feared Binger would become another Cold Springs if Jefferson and I couldn't bring things to an end soon. Tonight. Now.

We were about a hundred yards from the hill when we heard them, the sounds of their mounts' hoof beats almost keeping time with the drums, moving toward us from the southwest. Jefferson guided us off the trail leading up the hill and into a little stand of sugar maples and black oak. We sat our horses in the darkness. I shifted in my saddle and waited, silent and still, until the riders came into view.

It was a ten-trooper patrol of cavalry, led by the sergeant who had escorted us off the grounds of Fort Cobb in what seemed like another lifetime. They started up the rise toward us. Jefferson reached into his vest pocket for the makings and rolled himself a smoke, calm as could be. I'd never seen Jefferson smoke before, had no idea he carried around tobacco and paper. We waited until the sergeant's horse was pointed right at us and then struck a lucifer, lighting up the entire area around us in a red-yellow glow. The file of troopers made right for us, Sergeant Perkins stopping his horse a dozen feet away.

"Sergeant," Jefferson said, slow and easy. He was rolling another, balancing the rifle across the saddle while nimble fingers added tobacco to paper and rolled it closed. He gave it a lick to seal it and offered it out. "Smoke?"

Sergeant Perkins nudged his horse forward. With a nod, he took the coffin nail from Jefferson's fingers as his men, most of them little more than boys, fanned out and looked around nervously, searching for the invisible drummers, no doubt. "Thank you, sir." He lit his off Jefferson's, handed it back and straightened in his saddle, a his free hand near the butt of his revolver, belted high and in the cross-draw cavalry fashion. "Might I ask what you two gents are doing out here?"

"Well, we seem to have lost a photographer from back east, as well as a local man named Trevor Halfmoon. But mostly, we've come kill a right big old snake." Jefferson took a long drag off his cigarette and then smiled around the smoke he exhaled. "Want to come along?"

Sergeant Perkins blinked and sat back in his saddle. "I'm *supposed* to be patrolling the area until Captain Haskell shows up, and then my patrol is *supposed* to join his and sweep the area for the drummers." He took another drag off the own cigarette. "How big a snake are we talking about?"

"About the size of five strong men," I said softly.

The sergeant shook his head. "I don't want to call you a liar, sir, but I find that hard to believe."

Jefferson nodded. "I understand, Sergeant. I'll tell you what. If I can show you where the Spanish iron door is on this hill, will you and your men be willing go inside with me and face that snake? Because the door is a damned old tall tale, right? And if I can prove the door is actually real, then who's to say the giant-snake isn't real?"

I could see the sergeant mulling over what Jefferson had offered. I could see him thinking that if the door were real, then the gold might be real, and he still didn't believe any old tale about a snake five times bigger than a man. "If what you say is true, why should I risk my patrol against such a monster?"

"Is it not your job to protect the local settlers and tribes from danger?"

The sergeant nodded. "I understand you were once a soldier?"

"Yes. And later a United States Marshal, a police captain in San Francisco, and now a special agent of the federal government by appointment of President Harrison."

When Jefferson laid it out like that, I realized he's spent his entire life fighting for things he believed in and defending people from danger. I shook my head and wondered how he'd managed to survive to be over fifty years old.

The sergeant must have been as impressed as I was. "I and my men will follow you, sir. If what you say is true, the locals need to be protected." He paused and grinned, whiskers bristling. "Besides, how could I pass up a chance to take on a real monster, eh?"

Jefferson smiled back. "We'll need to picket the horses and place a guard or two on them. If we're going into the hill, we probably won't need the horses."

"And we don't want anyone coming along and thinking they're here for the takin'," the sergeant agreed. "I'll find us a likely spot." He turned and rode toward the hill. Jefferson and I trailed after.

"You sure about this, Jefferson?"

He frowned over at me. "If that snake-god monster sends a whole pack of snakes after us, we're going to need every fighting hand we can muster. We can't do this alone, Bill. At least these boys are soldiers."

I couldn't argue with him. I followed as Jefferson rode forward toward the head column of riders. I dropped back and let him ride side-by-side with the sergeant, the two exchanging histories of past campaigns, commanders, and units. I glanced over at the trooper next to me. He looked barely old enough to shave, which did nothing to reassure me that he and his comrades would stand and fight when faced with the snake-god. Partway up the hill, the sergeant raised his hand for the column to stop, and I rode up closer to Jefferson.

There on the path ahead of us was an opening in the side of the hill, right where Priscilla and I had tracked the beast and then lost it as it disappeared into the side of the hill. Sitting around the opening, partially hidden by the darkness, was a group of a dozen or so elders from the local tribes, men and women both, dressed in a mix of traditional clothing of their clans and the current fashion of the white settlers. They stood near the entrance around the door, a crudely made thing of iron and steel, about four feet tall, which had been pried away from the hill and set aside. I could see the hex signs, similar to the ones Granny Coulton had placed on barns and my rifle, but different enough that I couldn't read them. I felt my blood chill as the sense of broken magic washed over me.

I dismounted my horse and walked toward the door. Jefferson and Sergeant Perkins were speaking with some of the elders, but I wasn't listening to their words. A nearly toothless old man stepped aside, and a woman with steel gray coloring her black hair nodded in greeting at my approach. I stood before the opening, the musky smell of snake and dark damp earth filling my nose. Standing next to the door, which I saw was paper thin, I took a moment to marvel that the Spanish priests and soldiers had created such a thing while fighting the horror within.

"Can you repair the door?" I asked the woman.

She gave me a cool, appraising look, reminding me of my old granny with her steely gaze and steady demeanor. She nodded her head, a short, sharp gesture. "Yes, if Halfmoon can be brought out. Then we would have the blood of a Spaniard of the old magic to add to the closing. His family has the blood in their veins."

I glanced at her. It always came down to blood. The Sharps rifle warmed in my hands. "What else do you need?"

"The blood of whoever opened it. That person and their descendants shall become the keepers of this curse, with the power to hold the door firmly shut against future attempts to release the monster into an unsuspecting world."

"We strive against those who would summon Snake-That-Fell to walk the earth," I heard one of the elders say in a voice as old as the bones of the earth. I turned my attention away from the door and the opening. "With the seal broken, we are barely strong enough to slow Snake-That-Fell. Soon He will come, all in His fullness. Not the feeble creature that has slipped through the cracks of silence when called to devour a handful of humans and animals before returning to His slumber, but the true Snake-That-Fell will rise, and there are not enough midnights left to banish Him. He comes soon, and all who are not His children shall be swallowed."

The old woman swayed on her feet as she spoke in the *Kadohadacho* language. The drumming became louder and more frantic, as if scores of drummers had joined the others in the night and begun to close on the hill. The faces of the young cavalrymen looked pale and frightened in the light of the full moon shining overhead. Sergeant Perkins was silent, alternating his glances between the elders and the open door, and I wondered how much of the tale he was starting to believe.

"I'm going in," Jefferson said. He worked the bolt on his rifle, and the weapon whined and hummed. I checked my own weapon, the stock radiating warmth. "I won't ask anyone to come with me, but I sure would like to have a few folks watching my back."

"Can't we just set the door back?" Sergeant Perkins asked.

"No," I told him. "We've got people in there, and we need at least one of them to seal the door. We have to go in and fetch them."

Sergeant Perkins nodded and turned to his men. "I want five volunteers. The rest will stay near the door and wait for us to either come out or else carry a message back to the fort when we don't." Five young men stepped forward, obviously frightened but filled with the kind of foolish bravery only the young know.

The elders handed us short wooden torches and, with a few strikes of Jefferson's matches, we had illumination for the insides of the hill. Jefferson took the lead; the sergeant followed carrying a torch in one hand and a pistol in the other. I was third in line. The rest of the troopers, two more carrying torches, followed.

It was as if the little red-dirt hill were a mighty mountain on the inside. It seemed we wandered through a series of corridors and turns, nearly lost in an impossible fortress maze. Behind me I heard the fearful mutterings of the soldiers, and once I chanced a glance toward the ceiling only to find myself looking into an impossible night sky populated by stars and constellations I didn't recognize. The air lay heavy, filled with the smoke of our torches, the smell of dirt and rock, and the heavy, nauseating musk of snake with undertones of blood. The one constant was the drumming, for no matter how far or long we walked, the staccato rhythm that had greeted us outside the fill now filled the very earth, a constant, low rumble that permeated the rocks and vibrated into our bodies. Through it all we followed Jefferson, who was unwavering in his search for Halfmoon and Brinkerhoff. Rounding a sharp turn, we found the first of our missing comrades.

Halfmoon sat on the floor, eyes open, but the color in them gone, replaced by a milky white, as if he had seen the most terrible sight imaginable and needed his eyes no more. His hands were bloody and mangled, leaving smears on the wall where he drummed the same rhythm as those outside. He did not falter in his drumming, nor in any way acknowledge our approach.

The area here was wide enough for us to more from our previous single- and double-file march, and there was a branch in the path. We would have to choose which direction to travel. I knelt down next to Halfmoon as the sergeant gave soft orders to his men to secure the area and Jefferson moved to study the wreckage of what had to be Brinkerhoff's camera.

"Trevor. Trevor Halfmoon. Can you hear me?" I said softly. He turned his milk-white eyes toward me but said nothing. I took his face in my hand and held him steady. "Trevor Halfmoon, I have to know. Did you open the door? Did you touch it and move it away from the hill?"

"Yes," he whispered. "Yes."

I looked up to find Jefferson watching us. "I need to get him out of here, Jefferson. I think…I think the elders can seal that door, but they need Halfmoon."

"And when did you start knowing so much about magic, Bill?"

"My family, my whole family from way back can work magic. I can a little, enough to help start a campfire on a wet night or drive bugs from a bed I'm going to sleep in. This is magic beyond anything I've ever seen, but one of the elders said they needed Halfmoon's blood to seal the door."

Jefferson nodded. "Good enough. You take Halfmoon, Brinkerhoff's camera, and as many men as you think you need. I'm going to push on a little bit longer and see whether I can save Brinkerhoff or not." He pointed toward the side corridor. "One of the boys said there's a light down at the end of this corridor, dim, but there. The smells are stronger, too. I figure to go that way."

"I don't like leaving you," I said, though I was already lifting the unresisting Halfmoon to his feet. One of the soldiers had gathered up the camera.

"You two might be the only thing that stops the snake-god from getting loose." He paused. "The old ones outside said someone was trying to call the monster forth. I'm guessing it's someone from over at Hennessey Corner. You may have to find them and stop them at the source."

"I figured as much. Jefferson, if you don't find Brinkerhoff right quick, you need to get out. I ain't going to let them seal you up in here." I stood and took all of Halfmoon's weight. A soldier went to his other shoulder. I would be taking two men with me, leaving Jefferson with Sergeant Perkins and three troopers to deal with whatever lay at the end of the corridor.

"You may have to."

"Only if the big old snake is coming right for the door, and even then I might just try to bash it with my rifle." I grinned at him. "Besides, I don't want to have to explain to your widow why I shut you in a hill with a snake-god. So get your damned ass out of here before it comes to it."

"Fair enough," Jefferson said. "See you outside."

The delirious Halfmoon clinging to my shoulder, we started back out of the hill. We had gone two steps when I heard Halfmoon muttered, "Beware the children of the fallen God."

I looked over my shoulder to pass the warning to Jefferson and watched as a creature twice the size of a man, with a boy-child's face and body in the image of the snake-god, flowed from the dark shadows and ripped one of the troopers across the shoulder with his claws. I drew my colt and fired as the man screamed. The others wheeled to face the attack, gunshots loud in the enclosed space. The abomination made a pained mewing noise and collapsed in a heap, clawing at the ground a few time before growing still.

"Oh, God," one of the young soldiers whispered as another was loudly sick.

Jefferson gave me a stern look and waved the injured soldier to take the place of the one helping me with Halfmoon. "Jefferson—"

He turned away toward the dim-lit corridor, rifle steady. "You tell the elders to get that door ready to seal. We'll be right out."

I took my injured party and fled as fast we could all stumble, toward the cool Oklahoma night air blowing fresh through the caverns.

TEN

Violeta's warning came none too soon and barely in time for us to react. It was a testament to the abilities of Marshals Thomas and Reeves that the citizens of Binger, settlers and immigrants or the natives of the land, managed to get any who could not fight to safety while preparing for a ragged defense of the village. The young captain formed up his men in a calm and determined manner, detailing a corporal well into his middle years to assist the elder Mr. Halfmoon in organizing a rough kind of skirmish line.

I extolled Violeta to join the group seeking sanctuary in the church, which she did without argument and in a manner a too docile for my peace of mind, the more so since she carried her rifle over her uninjured shoulder. I asked Marshal Reeves to please watch for her safety, as I feared she would fling herself, wounded and weak, into the combat at some moment of her own choosing. For myself, I retreated to the hotel, where I could watch the battle from my window and wait to see if my unique skills might be needed. Waited to see if the wolf within would be called upon this night.

They entered the village down the main street from Hennessey Corner, a group of thirty or so traveling on foot. The walked on two legs like men, had the bodies of men and women, and were indeed dressed as such, but their heads, male and female both, were hairless, noses little more than nostril slits, skin covered with green and gray scales that glittered in the weak lights of street lanterns and the full moon overhead, designed to camouflage them in the grasses and trees, no doubt.

I recognized the preacher Jacob by the manner of his dress and thought one of the females to be the same one Violeta had subdued and stolen clothing from. They were led by a lizard man who wore the blue uniform of a federal soldier and strode along tall and proud as if he were about to conquer all he surveyed, sword and pistol at his side. Most of them carried three or four snakes on their shoulders, large diamond-backed rattlesnakes swelling the ranks of our potential enemies, all of them agitated and rattling warnings of impending violence. The snake or lizard people also carried weapons, rifles and pistols mostly, and they sported sharp-looking claws on the end of scaled hands. Others carried torches, flaming and glowing in the night, and those torches filled me with dread and fear that they meant to burn down the entire village as they had meant to burn the McHenry farm.

They fanned out along the streets, positioning themselves to best advantage against the defenders entrenched in the saloons, hotel, and jail. Their leader glared at Captain Haskell, who firmly held the reins to his nervous horse, flanked by two troopers to either side.

By orders of both Captain Haskell and Marshal Thomas, our defenders were forced to hold off their actions until the lizard-folks' intentions were known, though I would have preferred to have taken the initiative. They passed a long series of moments where neither side moved, and the smell of fear in the human defenders was strong enough to fill my still-human nose, until at last Captain Haskell broke the silence. "I do not know what your business is here tonight, but I should warn you that I and my men are prepared to defend this town."

"And if I ordered you to stand down, captain?" the one in the blue uniform hissed. He tossed his arms wide as if he might encircle them about the entire village. "Stand down, Haskell. Set aside your weapons and join me. Join us."

Preacher Jacob stepped forward. "Join my Lord and Master at this beginning of a new day, for He shall walk upon the earth again this very night and bring blessing upon His children and remake the world in His image. Join Him this night and know His glory!"

I could hear the frightened murmurs of the villagers, could almost taste the terror filling their hearts and souls.

"I do not know what you are, sir, except that you are not human. While you may once have been Colonel Rattinger, I fear you are no longer the man I served." Captain Haskell sat up straight in his saddle, his horse calming under his steady hand. "Leave now. This is your only warning."

The smile that stretched across the face of the one called Colonel Rattinger was hideous to behold, filled with gleaming teeth, sharp and pointed. He held the smile for an instant and then leapt toward Captain Haskell, covering the length of over twenty paces in a single bound as he drew the saber at his side.

That smile was enough warning for Captain Haskell, whose revolver was drawn and firing even as the colonel reached the apex of his leap.

The entire village erupted into violence. The lizard folk, though badly outnumbered, seemed sturdier that their human opponents and could withstand injures fatal to a human. I watched for a double handful of seconds as the defenders were quickly pushed back into an ever-tightening ring around the saloons and jail. The cavalry harassed the lizard folk from horseback, thinning the number of attackers, but the soldiers' own numbers were dwindling too quickly. As I feared would happen, a handful of buildings had been set ablaze. The flames from houses, the cotton mill, and the post office cast the street in a demonic glow. Panicked villages attempted to flee from the buildings, only to be cut down ruthlessly by their faster and hardier attackers.

I could no longer hold back and watch the slaughter. Undressing quickly, I shifted to my wolf form and bounded down the stairs, past the startled defenders and out a broken window. With one leap I landed on the back of a lizard man dressed in the clothes of a farmer, ripped his throat out, and chose my next target, the woman who had been told to poison me. She cut a small gash on my shoulder with her wicked claws, but she was no match for my speed and teeth, and she fell to the red-dirt street with a muted cry and a spray of crimson. The urge to kill sang in my blood as the full moon shone down from the sky above. I slayed two more with ease and howled my delight.

My delight turned to dread as the Colonel Rattinger, riddled with bleeding wounds, sliced off the head of the dismounted Captain Haskell with his gleaming saber. The captain's dead body collapsed, and I could feel the fight within the village defenders fail, the smell of fear rushing into my nose even as three of the lizard folks converged on me and the village burned.

"Run, fools!" Colonel Rattinger stood in the middle of the street over the fallen Captain Haskell. "Run, but there is nowhere for you to hide from Him. Even now the summoning fires are lit. We are the future of this world. Join us as His children or become no more than cattle to be—"

The roar of a heavy rifle was followed by the explosion of Colonel Rattinger's head into a bloody gray mess. The body pitched forward to rest next to Captain Haskell. There was a long moment of silence, followed by a second roar. Another of the lizard folk went down to a bullet through the head. The battle turned with the death of the apparent leader of the lizard-folk as the villagers took courage. They also began shooting at the lizard folks' heads.

The three charging me changed their direction, rushing toward the church, where I knew in my heart Violeta had taken up a position in the bell tower and was now raining death on the creatures below. I turned to follow them, determined to protect my friend and everyone else within the building.

Marshals Thomas and Reeves stood at the top of the steps, fighting as if possessed, pistols smoking, a ring of dead snakes and lizard people around them. Thomas was reloading as Reeves, a pistol in each hand, met the change, killing with cool precision. His hammer fell on an empty and he drew his long knife even as I crashed into the final attacker—Preacher

Jacob— knocking him flat and tearing out the back of his neck.

With their two leaders suddenly down, the other creatures began a panicked retreat away from the village, running and bounding into the night.

I sat on my haunches in the dirt, watching as the villagers rushed to draw water from wells, the creek, and the train water tower in a heroic attempt to save their homes and businesses. The ragged survivors of the cavalry troop and Mr. Halfmoon's volunteer rifle squad gathered in the streets, captured errant horses, and organized. I turned at a sound from behind me in the church. I gazed up at...at...a familiar-smelling form holding a rifle.

Violeta. Yes. Violeta.

Smell of blood strongly...

My maid. My friend.

Crunch of fresh and bones under my teeth...

Violeta...

Musky snake...

Oh...

Taste of the blood and scales...

Oh. My William... I am so...

Past the swaying bleeding bleating braying things before me the fleeing snake-taste blood dripping fear running running running into the night...

William...

I lifted my head and howled long and loud, freezing the ones before me. I growled once at them and then raced away into the night, seeking more prey under the silver glow of the moon above.

ELEVEN

Glancing over my shoulder, I made sure Sergeant Perkins and his men were still with me. The sergeant seemed like a solid sort of veteran. I'd served with men like him before, the kind of lifetime soldier and professional non-commissioned officer that could be counted on to reliably stick out even the nastiest battle while doing his dead-level best to ensure the young officers and new privates didn't die of stupid. Or at least, no more of them than necessary in any given battle. I'd been a dumb young officer once, one lucky enough to have a man like Sergeant Perkins serving under me.

The troopers, though, all looked young and green and frightened. Perkins had probably chosen them for the night patrol to get a little experience under their belts in what he thought would be low-risk patrol, even if it was at night. I'd have preferred it if he'd chosen his troopers for experience instead, but there it was. I had a veteran sergeant and three beardless boy-soldiers to watch my back.

I'd have traded the whole lot for Bill Blenchy instead. Hell, I'd've liked to have Lady Priscilla right now as well. I could use a good wolf tracker. After a moment I had the ungracious thought that Violet might be steadier in a fight than most of the young'uns behind me. Ungracious maybe, but also the hard truth. I could wish all I wanted, but Bill needed to get Halfmoon out of the hill and try to work whatever witchery he knew to seal the damned door, and I needed Lady Priscilla and her wolf to guard Binger.

I left the Tesla rifle slung over my shoulder. If the lesser creatures could be stopped by normal lead bullets, I wanted to save my rifle for the real monster. I eased closer to the light and hoped I didn't get my fool-self killed. Millie would never forgive me if I did. I lifted a hand behind me to stop the troops and signaled Perkins to get to the other side of the opening. He took three troopers and dashed to the opposite wall. I peered inside the opening, looking down at the scene below in disgust.

The chamber was impossibly large for the size of the hill we had entered. I gave Perkins a quick check and could see he was thinking the same as I as he beheld the cavern below. The size of the cavern was disconcerting enough, but the stench was almost too much: musk and blood and bile and shit. I lifted the bandana around my neck up to cover my nose and mouth, yet this awful reek paled against the unimaginable horror that dwelled within.

It sat upon a throne cut from the red rock of the hill, the size of five large men, wings tucked behind its scale-covered body. Over a dozen smaller versions of itself surrounded the throne, all of them with human faces: men, women, boys, and girls. The monster had changed them somehow. Some dark and putrid magic had turned these poor human settlers into winged monsters, no doubt the children Halfmoon had muttered about in his fevered state. At the base of the throne lay the unmoving form of Nicolaas Brinkerhoff. I couldn't tell if the photographer was alive or dead from this vantage.

Stretched out on a stone slab, no more than ten feet from the throne, was woman not yet changed to one of the monsters. She wore the plain dress of a farmwife, the garment torn at her shoulders and along her stomach, which I could see even from here was swollen with child. She was covered in sweat and occasionally gave a small moan as she twisted in pain on the harsh stone bed.

I'd come for Brinkerhoff, but I would have cursed and retreated given the odds and the fact that he appeared dead. Maybe I should have. Maybe I should have taken my small force and retreated, but that option was no longer viable. I couldn't retreat and leave that woman and her unborn babe to the mercy of those things below.

I waved Perkins over. "You see her?"

"Yup. We're going to do something mighty stupid and try to rescue her, aren't we?"

"You think you can reach her if the boys and I set down some cover fire?"

"You want me to run down in there amongst them?"

"You scared?"

"Yes, sir. I am."

"Fair enough. I don't see any way one of us could sneak past all that mess and get her out alive. We could just charge in shooting. I'm pretty sure this rifle of mine will hurt that big old snake-god, and we'd have surprise on our side. I reckon the troopers would get a few before they could react." I paused. "Will you do it?"

"Yes, sir, though I'm worried about the boys breaking and running when those things get themselves sorted and start fighting back. "

"Scared boys tend to shoot."

"As long as they don't shoot one of us by accident," he muttered

It took too long to set up for my taste. Perkins handed his rifle over to one of the three troopers who would be staying at the entrance and providing cover fire, taking the youngster's pistol in exchange for his Winchester.

"We could try to lure them out to us," one of the troopers whispered.

"Better to knock 'em down from ambush," I answered.

"The captain has the right of it," Perkins said.

"You ready?" I asked him

"Hell no. But I'm going to do it anyway."

I'd learned long ago that if you had surprise and enough rifles and held the high ground, the best thing to do was rain lead down until your opponent stopped moving. The problem was that Sergeant Perkins would be charging into the bloody middle of that rain of fire. It would be too easy for us to go down under our own men's bullets, but damned if I could see any other way to get that woman out of the snake-god's den.

I lifted the Tesla rifle to my shoulder and took a bead on the snake-god. Everyone with a rifle would pick a target and open fire, and then it would be move forward, fire, move forward, fire until we either met our objectives or were forced to retreat.

"Fire." The word passed softly over my lips.

The roar of the Winchesters in the enclosed space was counterpointed by the soft pop of my own rifle, and three of the creatures collapsed to the ground as the snake-god was blown against the back of his red rock throne by the force of my weapon's energy. We charged and fired again. A few of the scaled creatures that had fallen rose, and others fell under our surprise onslaught. It was the last coordinated volley we would fire.

They came at us fast, claws extended and attacking from all directions, screeching as if they were the very hounds of hell. The snake-god rose from his throne and gave a roar, which caused the rifle fire around me to wither and falter. It took all of my courage to not drop my weapon and fall to my knees before the great snake. With shaking hands, I lifted the rifle and fired again. He took a step backward, the spell of his awful presence broken. A great scorch mark marred the monster's hide.

Sergeant Perkins leapt into the middle of the lesser creatures, both Colts blazing away as he fought his way to the prone woman. It was enough to spur the men to greater effort, and the rifle fire intensified even as the smaller creatures scratched and leapt, flew and slashed at our flesh. A warning yell made me turn to my left. I fired, and the winged, scaled body with the screaming face of a little girl exploded under the impact, bloody bits spraying across the chamber.

There was a single startled moment of silence before the snake-god reared and roared again, reaching out with long arms and wicked talons to snatch one of the young soldiers who had charged too close. He lifted the hapless man and with gleaming fangs and bit the torso and ripped it in half, flinging the torn body at one of his comrades, who ducked. I fired at the snake-god, missing, sending rocks and debris falling from the roof of the cavern. It shook its massive head and lashed out at another trooper, killing both the man and one of its own creations.

Sergeant Perkins ran past me, screaming to retreat and carrying the unconscious woman over his shoulders. Retreat seemed like a sensible idea. I managed to get the other surviving trooper moving, and we battled out way toward the exits. Our little band fled the cavern, the creatures snapping at our heels. I slammed a fresh magazine into my rifle and slung it over my shoulder. It seemed like the snake-god's bulk wouldn't allow him to chase us down the narrow passages, and I was willing to trust my Schofield to deal with his lesser but still dangerous children.

We ran. Make no mistake, we ran as if the devil himself was chasing us, which he might well have been. We ran from the snake god, ran from his twisted children. Ahead we heard the faint sounds of drumming, growing louder even as I looked over my shoulder to see the last trooper snatched by clawed hands. He screaming once, shrill and high as he was dragged back into the darkness. The scream cut off with a wet ripping noise.

Somehow the snake-god was still coming for us, moving through the narrow tunnels, the walls seeming to bend and twist about his body as he moved. I unslung my rifle and squeezed the trigger, firing into the monster's face. I didn't wait to see if I had done any damage. I followed the sergeant, running as hard as I could manage on tired old legs. I turned a corner and found Sergeant Perkins sprawled on the dirt floor, his chest ripped open. The woman was in an untidy heap on next to him, as if he had been torn apart and simply dropped her as he died. One of his revolvers lay next to his out-flung hand, the other near the quivering and sobbing farmwife.

Nicolaas Brinkerhoff—or what was once Brinkerhoff—stood over the dead sergeant, crimson blood dripping from its talons. Brinkerhoff's coat and shirt were torn where the small leathery wings had burst through. He gave them a flap as he regarded me with his bright yellow snake eyes. He hissed, his tongue tasting the air. He jumped over the farm wife, screaming as he sailed toward me.

I lifted the rifle and squeezed the trigger. The weapon gave a soft pop, and the green light struck Brinkerhoff in midflight. The impact of the energy ripped through the man-monster's chest, painting the corridor with blood and internal organs. Brinkerhoff's ruined corpse landed at my feet. For a moment I stood looking at the dead man-monster, filled with the knowledge that I failed the photographer as surely as I had failed so many in Cold Springs. I should have known the damned fool would come back here. I should have gotten here sooner, dealt with the Tesch boys quicker, gone into the hill hours ago. I should have done *something*.

I held the rifle steady as the gibbering, howling, screeching noises grew ever closer and the drumming seemed to become louder, vibrating the very rocks of the hill. I wished it was easier to switch from rifle to pistols. I doubted I'd have the time to reload the rifle with all the monsters in the world bearing down on me, and I hated to waste the rifle ammo in something I could kill with lead. But I had no idea what was coming, and I wanted the rifle in my hand for the snake-god himself.

The first of them burst from the darkness around the bend in the corridor, a snarling, angry, taloned thing with the head of a bearded man. I fired the rifle, reminding myself that it was no longer a man, or at least I prayed nothing of the man still dwelt inside the beast. The energy bullet struck true, and the thing exploded. The ones coming behind pulled up short in sudden fear. The drumming increased in volume and tempo. I fired twice more, destroying another, but I knew I was down to my last cartridge, and I didn't have time to reload a fresh magazine. I fired the final round and transferred the rifle to my left hand, drawing my Schofield and hoping the snake-god didn't show up.

"Get down!" I heard Bill Blenchy yell behind me. I dropped to the floor as a barrage of rifle fire, including Blenchy's Sharps, filled the narrow corridor. The attacking snake-monsters fled under the onslaught.

I rose up as they retreated. "Good to see you, Bill." He had three soldiers and a couple of the local natives with him. They were carrying lanterns. They pulled up short when they saw the weapon in my hand and the body behind me. I pointed at the soldiers. "You two! Get that woman out of here." They paused for a moment and then did as I told them, their training to listen to orders overriding the dawning terror in their eyes. They snapped to attention for a second before helping the woman up and half carrying, half dragging her toward the exit. "Can we get out of here now?" I asked Blenchy.

The look on his face filled me with dread. "Nope. They need a few more minutes to seal the door. Figured I'd best come find you and warn you before they closed the hill up for good."

"I appreciate that." Around us the drumming settled into a rhythm that made it hard not to simply stand in place and sway. Down the corridor, we heard the sounds of the creatures gathering themselves for another run at us. I thumbed cartridges from my pocket into the rifle's empty magazine and snapped it back into place. I had those five and three more I could put into the empty magazine in my pocket. Eight rounds to fight the snake-god. I didn't much care for those odds. "How long before they can seal the door?"

"Not long," Blenchy said, peering over his shoulder at the darkness. "Can you hold the entrance against Snake-That-Fell while I help them finish?"

I slammed the magazine home and worked the rifle's bolt. The weapon gave a low whine as I placed myself in front of the entrance to the hill. "I'll hold it. Do I get a little help?"

"Yup. Private Fulton and Mr. Washington here have volunteered," Blenchy said as he slung his own rifle over his shoulder. "When I call out, you better come running through that door. I don't know how fast they'll need to close it to make the magic stick."

"You just remember to call out."

He gave my shoulder a squeeze, and I turned with my two allies to face the darkness and the monsters within.

I exited the red rock hill into the cool night air to the sounds of drumming so loud and intense it shook my bones and my heart struggled join the rhythm. I could feel the magic in the air, taste it on my tongue, sharp and metallic instead of the earthy taste I had come to know as my Granny Coulton or the dark, smoking taste of magic when I worked it myself.

Halfmoon sat against the hill near the door, his bloody hands wrapped up in bits of cloth one of the elders had provided. At the base of the hill were a handful of campfires belonging to a collection local tribes, the likes of which I had never seen gathered before: Caddo, Wichita, Arapaho, Keechi, Kiowa, Comanche, Cherokee, Creek, Osage, Ponca, Quapaw...I spotted others by their manner of dress and decoration; a gathering for the ages. There were drummers from all the groups and enough armed fighters to hold off the cavalry from Fort Cobb so they could finish whatever they were about.

The ancient Caddo woman told me they would set the binds around it, but I had to place the door before they sealed it with Halfmoon's blood. They all refused to touch the door itself.

They would anchor the door to Trevor Halfmoon and all the Halfmoon line thereafter. Not only had he broken the seal, setting himself as the focus of ruined magic, but the hill had tasted his blood, had drunk it into the soil as he drummed his hands to bloody ruins inside the darkness. The bones of the earth would respond to him. It was about the blood. It was always about the blood. I heard Jefferson and others fighting and firing and wanted to join them, to take part in a battle I understood, but I was needed here.

Two of the elders helped Halfmoon rise to his feet. "You understand what's about to happen? You and your family will have the charge of keeping Snake That Fell bottled up in this hill. The blood of your family will be responsible for the monster's prison. You and your family will become the keepers of the curse within." The Caddo woman's voice was ice cold.

"I understand," Halfmoon said, though I suspected he didn't. That was the way of it with magic. There would be price, one none of us could even begin to guess at, one that would reveal itself in time and God help us all if the family line died out and there was no left to guard the door.

"Then unwrap your hands and place them on the door."

He did as she bid with the elders' assistance. She reached out and took his left hand, drew one of the knives from his belt, and placed it in his ruined right hand. "Blood is the price." He cut his left palm, letting it fill with blood. I took his left wrist and forced his bleeding hand onto the door, guiding it along the hex marks. The blood smoked, and there was a soft sizzling sound. Halfmoon gasped and swayed, but the elders held him upright. "Blood is paid. Blood seals and blood binds." As the old woman's words faded, I felt my own magic stir.

As his hands passed over the last of the marks, Halfmoon screamed, his eyes rolled up, and his body went limp. The Caddo woman let go of his wrist and nodded to the elders. They gently set him down on the ground to wait for the last bit of the ritual. I picked up the door—it might be made of metal, bit it was wafer-thin and lighter than it looked—and set it in the opening of the hill. All I needed to do now was close the door, hammer it into the hill, and then let the elders trace half moon symbols at each corner. That would take time, and I feared Snake That Fell would push his way past the door before we could seal it. That was part of the drummers' responsibility, to hold off the snake-god, but other powerful magic was calling the monster awake, had weakened the previous seal enough that the monster had been able to walk out of the hill-prison, as least for short times, and was even now calling the creature.

Leaving the door set just off the entrance, I picked up my rifle and nodded to the old Caddo woman. "Jefferson! Come on out!" Nothing. I'd been afraid of this. I poked my head into the dark cavern. A weird green light flared, followed by a roar. Jefferson at least was still alive.

Private Fulton crawled out of the entrance, his eyes wide and wild. "It slithers. It…claws…fangs in the darkness. From the walls blood flows green…"

Sure I would get nothing from the wounded and delirious man, I stepped back into the hill, ready to either retrieve Jefferson or spend my last few minutes fighting the thing within before death and darkness claimed me.

I wished I could tell Priscilla…well, I wished I could tell her a lot of things, but she already knew what I would say.

Once more unto the breach, dear friends, once more.

\#

We could hear them, scuttling and shuffling in the darkness. I leaned the Tesla rifle against the side of the corridor and checked both my pistols. I had enough rounds on my belt to reload the Schofield a few times, but once the Colt was empty the old ball and cap revolver was useless. I dropped the smaller revolver into my left trouser pocket, checked the rifle again, and hoped Bill and then elders got whatever witchery they were up to done in a hurry.

They came on in a wild charge, scaled bodies shimmering in the dim light of lanterns, stubby, useless wings flapping, the once-human faces twisted up in pain or fury, screaming. Our weapons echoed and roared in the close confines of the cave, and three of the creatures went down, only to rise again and continue the charge. I had almost emptied my Schofield before they broke off the attack. I snapped the revolver open and reloaded, my hands working automatically from decades of practice.

They attacked in a second wave, driven by the monster following them. The Snake-God, looking impossibly large in the narrow confines of the cave, strode behind, each of his steps taking up as much ground as five of theirs, the rock of the cave bending and warping impossibly at his passage. My companions stopped firing as I lifted the rifle and fired at the giant monster's chest. The green energy bolt smashed against the scales, and it staggered backward. I fired again, screamed my own challenge, and charged at the snake-god, firing a third time as it backed away.

Behind me there was gunfire, and I thought I heard Blenchy's voice, but something in me screamed to press my attack, to drive the creature back to its lair before Bill sealed the door, that if I left it too strong and too close to the door, it might somehow break through. I fired at its head, striking it under the jaw in a burst of green energy. I bolted the last round into the chamber as the green light faded. I was left with the sudden realization that I had moved too far from the lanterns and now stood in darkness with a giant snake only yards away. I started backing out of the cave.

"Jefferson! Jefferson, where the hell are you?"

I chanced a quick glance over my shoulder. There was a dim light in the cave corridor, moving toward me.

The smell, hot, rancid, spoiled meat and rotting vegetables, made me turn back. I caught the barest shadowy movement, the yellow glint of a long fang in the lantern light moving toward me. I fired the rifle from my hip, angled upward. The cave lit up with the eerie green of the energy bullet for an instant, illuminating the snake-god's open mouth a few bare feet away from my head.

The force of the detonation flung me to my back and sent me skidding away from the creature. I heard a pained roar and a series of hissed words I didn't understand but which frozen the very marrow in my bones. With numbed fingers I ejected the empty magazine, fumbled for the last one filled with my final three rounds, and popped it into the rifle, working the bolt, my ears ringing and buzzing the whole time. Around me, bits of rock and sand gently, sporadically fell.

A touch on my shoulder made me turn. Bill Blenchy, rifle in hand, was saying something to me, but I couldn't hear him. What I could do was read the urgency in his eyes as he looked back toward the exit. I managed to climb up on wobbly legs, using the rifle as a crutch. I nodded toward him, and we started out of that cave, my ears still ringing. I could see the opening ahead. One of the elders, the old woman, pointed at something behind us, and I felt Bill stumble into me.

I spun around, ears ringing and head throbbing as the large talons lashed out. I pushed the already bleeding Blenchy to the ground, out of the way of the sweep of those wicked claws. I lifted the rifle and fired, the angry snake god and what remained of his children glowing green and demonic in my sight. I worked the bolt and fired again, this time into ceiling. The ground under me shook as earth rained down. I grabbed Blenchy and dragged him out of the cave as the ringing in my ears reached a high-pitched whine. I aimed at the roof of the cave and fired my last round, heavy earth collapsing with a satisfying crash. I shook my head as my hearing returned.

"Jefferson, get out of there!"

I did as Blenchy commanded, staggering from the cave mouth and looking around in surprise at the assembled tribes of the central Oklahoma Territory prairie surrounding the mountain. The drumming filled my now-returned hearing, and I slumped down on a handy bit of rock as Blenchy, bleeding across his back, set the door in place. Halfmoon rose to his feet and rubbed blood from his wounded hands on the corners of the door as the drumming and chanting reached an apex. There was an audible pop.

"It may not be enough," Blenchy said. "I've got to get down to Hennessey Corner and stop whoever's calling the creature out."

I nodded. "I'm not sure either of us are up for much more, but I'm with you." It had to be us. I could only imagine the disaster that would ensue if the small army of warriors from the Caddo, Wichita, and other tribes were to descend on Hennessey Corner looking to stop—well, I figured it was Granny Creswell for sure, and maybe Marshal Rich—but if they attacked the town and fighting broke out, they might massacre everyone in the heat of the moment and their panic over the snake-god. The response from Washington would be swift and violent. It had to be me and Bill.

Leaving Halfmoon in the capable hands of his elders, we set off for Hennessey Corner, riding through the night. The remaining young cavalry troopers had gathered their horses and, gaining the loan of a buckboard from one of the tribes, loaded up their wounded and the pregnant woman, heading for Binger and Doc Meaghan.

Blenchy and I were left to deal with the townsfolk. We rode through the night surrounded by the drumbeats echoing off Crying Woman and rolling down the dark prairie, the heavy thump-thump-thump at our backs the entire way, as if urging and pushing us onward. Above us, the full moon hung pale amidst a sea of stars suddenly gone strange, as if somehow we had ridden our ponies into another world. If Bill was concerned or had noticed the unfamiliar constellations, he gave no indication. Given his injuries and the paleness of his face, I suspected his focus was on staying in the saddle.

We found the main road from Crying Woman to Hennessey Corner, not so much a road as a wagon track for the farmers and drovers hauling cotton from the fields to the gins and on to the railroads. We urged our mounts to greater speed once we hit the well-worn track. We topped a rise at a gallop and below us lay the town. Most of the houses were dark, but at the crossroads all the buildings and business were lit up, as was the Creswell home. In the middle of the crossroads was a huge bonfire. I could just make out shapes moving in the village. And near the fire was a shape similar to the snake-god.

He was waiting for us in the middle of the road, as if someone had warned him we were coming. Whoever was working magic to release the snake-god might have known we were working against them out at Crying-Woman. Maybe they knew we were coming. My only real surprise was that he was alone. There was something ominous about Marshal Rich waiting on the road from Crying Woman and the darkness of the town. We slowed out horses to a walk.

"I could shoot him down from here," Blenchy said, one hand on the butt of his rifle.

"No. He wasn't one of them snake people in the photograph. We can't just go shooting people because we think they might be involved."

"He's between us and whoever's working that magic, and time is running out, Jefferson."

I couldn't argue with that. "Then ride on around him. If he draws on you, I'll charge him." I drew my Schofield and rested it across my lap in the saddle. "Go on. I'll meet you in town."

Blenchy nodded once and then kicked his horse, taking off away from Rich and circling around to the man's left, away from his gun hand. Marshal Rich would have to be something special to hit Blenchy at that range and speed. Rich watching Blenchy go for a few minutes, then turned to face me. I nudged my mustang, and we started forward at a walk, stopping about ten yards away from him, turning to present a narrow target while aiming my already drawn Schofield right at him.

"Agent Stottlemyre," he said softly.

"Marshal Rich," I answered. "I hope you don't mind if I ride on by."

"I can't let you do that, sir."

I frowned. "Of course you can. Blenchy's already down in the town. He's ready to stop whoever's up to the witchery and deal with the people responsible for all settlers and others who've disappeared or been killed. I don't know if you're part of all the stuff happening, but I'm giving you a chance to ride away."

"You don't understand, Agent Stottlemyre. This is the time, and there isn't any stopping it now. The best you can do is mess things up and make us lose control of The Great Serpent. I can't allow you to do that, and there are enough of us still in the town to deal with Mr. Blenchy."

"Some of you have left the town?"

He smiled. "The best of us, those closest to The Great Serpent, have gone to strike the first blow. Once we secure the rail at Binger and raise Him from his slumber, we'll deal with the fort."

"What do you get out of this?"

"A return to the natural order of things. Power. Revenge."

"Revenge?"

"For my family and my country."

"The war's over, Marshal."

"Never, sir. As long as true southern men and women stand firm, our great country will rise up again despite the aggression of the northern forces. The Great Serpent will give us something to rally around and the power we lacked to secure our independence."

The deep growl of Blenchy's rifle filled the night, echoing up from the town and over the drums beating their constant staccato. As if it were some kind of signal, Rich reached for his gun, even as more gunfire erupted from the town. I lifted the Schofield and fired twice before he cleared leather, kicking my mount to ride in a circle around him.

I fired twice more as he got off his first shoot. He swayed in the saddle and tried to turn to track me. I fired my last round as he fired again, and I heard his bullet whine past me. Dropping the empty Schofield into the holster, I drew the Colt from my pocket and kicked my horse into a charge, leaning over the mustang's neck for cover as I fired, closing the ten or so yards in seconds. Rich got off another shot and then toppled to the ground. I checked to see if he was moving. His chest was covered in blood, shirt stained dark in the pale moonlight. He blinked up at me once, then relaxed as death took him.

Tucking the Colt into my boot, I kicked the horse, urging it to best speed, reloading the Schofield from horseback as I had done so many times in the cavalry. I snapped it shut as I entered the town and rode to the crossroad.

Blenchy sat his horse, leaning over in exhaustion, rifle across his saddle. Marshals Thomas and Reeves, along with what I hoped was a posse of citizen from Binger, had surrounded a handful of people on foot. I noticed a few dead bodied on the street. Marshal Thomas looked up at me and nodded. A large black wolf raced past.

"Bill?" I asked.

"It's done. Whoever was doing the summoning broke and ran before I got here. I had to shoot a talisman in the snake-doll to stop the magic, but then it as easy enough to push the snake-doll into the fire. It's done," he said again, leaning farther forward in the saddle.

It took me a moment to register the blood dripping from Blenchy to his saddle and down onto the ground. I climbed off my mustang and ran over just as he lost his balance and started to pitch off his own mount. Marshal Thomas grabbed Blenchy's horse to keep it from bolting, and Reeves helped me ease the tall man to the ground. The wounds from the snake-god were worse than I'd thought.

"Priscilla..." he whispered. "I need..."

I didn't know what else to do, so I whistled. The large black wolf walked up to us, whining, and as I looked into her eyes, I wasn't sure Lady Priscilla Talbot was still there. Bill's eyes rested on the big she-wolf, and he frowned. "Priscilla...I need you."

###

I knew the man. Knew the smell of him, the smell of his blood. He called out in a voice that somewhere in my dimmest memories I associated with safety. Whining, I walked up to him, the smell of his blood strong in my nose. I knew him. I knew…William

My William.

He reached out a hand and touched my fur. I started to shy away, instinct telling me to run, flee, escape, not be caught, that men were not to be trusted, but the gentle touch awoke more memories in me, memories of a time when I was a woman.

"Priscilla." I understood his words, understood that Priscilla was my name. "I would look upon my love's face," he whispered.

The memories flooded forward then, of a time another man asked to see my face as he lay dying, and the sharp loneliness of his loss. I remembered grief. I remembered this man, William, gently paying me court, my joy at finding love with someone who understood and loved both the human Priscilla and the wolf. I remembered fighting creatures, and wild rides, and making love with William for the first time, both of us naked on blankets next to a campfire on the Russian plains. The wolf knew as well, knew this man was my mate. Our mate, for he loved us both. Unheeding of the people surrounding me, I surrendered to the human-within, changed, shifted, stretched, and grew. The night air was cool against my skin.

"William," I said softly. "Oh my, William."

I held him then, even as someone draped a blanket over my naked shoulders. William coughed and shuddered, and I heard a voice call for a wagon. Marshal Stottlemyre's gentle commands drew me from William, who had closed his eyes but was breathing. He was lifted into a wagon, and I settled next to him, holding his head in my lap. Reeves and Stottlemyre tried to keep pressure on his wounds.

I have few memories of the ride, except that it was cold and that every time the wagon jolted on a rut, William gave a little cry of pain. Once more Marshal Stottlemyre drew me away as four strong men carried William into the hotel and up to our room. I sat with Violeta, who was sleeping peacefully in her own bed, recovering from the injuries she received during our battle. At last Marshal Stottlemyre and Doctor Meaghan slipped into the room.

"He'll be all right, I think," the doctor said. "He's lost a lot of blood, and he's exhausted, but it doesn't look like anything critical was shot or stabbed. He's going to need rest. Weeks of rest, and when he's ready to start moving around, I want you to take him someplace warm and quiet for a couple of months to finish his recovery." The doctor smiled. "I appreciate all you've done for our town, but no heroics for a while."

I nodded my agreement, and the kindly old man slipped back out as silently as he had entered. I regarded Marshal Stottlemyre. "Is it done?"

He nodded. "Yeah. I had a talk with Granny Creswell."

"And?"

"I don't have enough to actually arrest her. She wasn't at the bonfire. No one'll testify against her. At best I could try to use Brinkerhoff's photograph, but a good lawyer would just argue it was a fake. It's one thing to get a person who saw it to believe in snake-men, but for someone who wasn't there..." He gave a shrug. "She said the stars wouldn't be right to try again for another half-century. I could try to make that into a confession—"

"It sounds like a confession to me."

"But would it to a judge and twelve men? You think that'll be enough for them to hang a little old lady? And I can't just kill her in cold blood."

"No."

"I'm sorry, Lady Priscilla."

"Priscilla," I said with a sigh. "And you have nothing to apologize for, Jefferson. William and Violeta both know how dangerous our work is."

He nodded. "True enough. Still, I was leading the team."

"Yes." I smiled at him. "We'd like you to keep leading."

He shook his head. "No. I'm too darned old, and I want to go home to my wife." He paused and frowned. "Marry him."

I frowned. "Jefferson… I can't give him children. The curse won't allow me to carry a child to term."

"You could have lost him. He could lose you. You both love each other something fierce. Marry the man."

I understood the wisdom of his words, and the wolf—my wolf—knew William as our mate. It was time to set aside my very British nobility complex and give William and myself what we wanted. "Will you stand with us?"

"Of course."

I smiled up at him. "Thank you. Now go get some rest."

He smiled. "A warm bed sounds like a fine thing." He nodded and left me alone.

I checked Violeta. She was sleeping soundly, peacefully. I tucked the blankets around her and then checked on William. He was less restful, but his breaths were deep and even, though he was sweating. I settled next to him, watching him sleep will listening with a wolf's ears. Finally I heard Jefferson beginning to snore softly from the room next door.

Rising carefully so as not to disturb William's slumber, I pulled on my boots and gathered my weapons before leaving the room. I had unfinished business this night. The night clerk was dozing, so I exited the hotel unchallenged. Dawn would be coming soon, and I wanted to be done with my task and back at the hotel before my companions awoke. In the stables, I chose a small black mare, found her tack, and saddled her myself, leaving behind a silver half-dollar for her rent.

The ride back to Hennessey Corner was quiet, and I took time to admire the flatlands: the cotton fields, the wildness of the place. In the distance a coyote howled. Another answered. I smiled at their antics. Were I of a more domesticated nature, I could see settling here. I was unsure what would happen to the people of Hennessey Corner, but that was a question for

Marshals Thomas and Reeves, who would be dealing with the aftermath. I only cared about one citizen of the village.

I stopped in front of her home. The door was unlocked and a light on in the parlor. I let myself in. Granny Creswell sat in a wooden rocker, a cup of tea near her hand. She looked up and frowned as I walked in.

"Hello," I said.

"What do you want, girl?" She didn't rise from the chair, and her hands were hidden under a quilt. I sniffed but didn't smell gun oil.

"I wanted to look upon the one who caused all this grief."

"Prove it."

"I can smell the guilt on you. You need to pay for what you've done, whether it can be proved or not. There will be consequences."

She snorted. "Get out of my home, girl. Go on. You're dealing with things you don't understand. There are not enough midnights left in the world. Eventually they'll all run out. You people might have stopped us this time, but the wheel turns, years pass, and I can afford to be patient. The Great Serpent will slumber for another fifty years, but we shall be ready to call him forth, and you people will have long gone to worms and dust. Go on back to your menfolk before you get hurt, girl, and live your little life." She snorted again. "Smell the guilt, indeed. I'm too old for such foolishness."

"No, really. I can smell the guilt." I let myself change a bit, bringing the wolf forward before relaxing back into my human skin. "And I can smell the magic."

"Who are you?" she asked, her eyes widening in surprise and no little fear.

"Someone who doesn't believe in chivalry or second chances." I stepped toward her as I opened my clutch purse. "Someone whose love was nearly killed because of you." I drew the bone-handled and silver-bladed knife I carried for monsters that could only die by the touch of that noble metal.

Monsters like myself. I smiled at her. "Someone who is a predator."

Later, I dropped my bloody dress on the floor and curled up around my William's warm, living body.

EPILOGUE

"Washington. I'd have never thought to see the day."

I smiled at Millie as she folded another dress and packed it in the steamer trunk. She'd been a bit flustered since I'd returned from Oklahoma Territory bearing new scars and wearing a new badge, her normal calm tossed out the door at all the change I brought home with me. I was wearing the badge on my vest even as I helped Millie pack. There was something pleasing about being "U.S. Special Services Agent #1."

I stayed in Binger for two more weeks after we defeated the cult of the snake-god, long enough for all of us to recover from our wounds sufficient to take a train back to San Francisco. Long enough to make sure Marshal Reeves had everything well in hand in Hennessey Corner, where he would be acting as the local law until the district judge in Arkansas was comfortable turning it back over the town.

Long enough to see my friends Bill and Priscilla properly married at last, exchanging the vows in the same church that had seen so much battle. There had been a scramble to find Bill a good suit to be married in, since the man had a tendency to ruin his clothing. We found him something suitable, and I had the honor and pleasure of standing with him.

Lady Priscilla had tried to eschew anything fancy for herself, but the local women were having none of that. If the two of the people who had fought to save Binger—in fact had fought to save the world—were to marry in their church, the townsfolk planned to do the wedding right. Pricilla looked lovely in the white dress the ladies constructed, a garland of prairie flowers on her head, her face covered by a veil gifted to her by what must had been the senior matriarch of the town. I'd had to nudge Bill to remind him to breathe when he first saw his bride.

I moved to a different room in the hotel after the wedding. To give them some privacy, of course.

"It'll be okay," I told Millie in a soft voice. "I've lived in Washington before. I know the town."

She cast me a long, measuring look before she returned to packing. I placed some of my own mementos in the crate for the cross-country move: medals, ribbons, documents, and other bits of my past.

Our wounded but merry band had traveled to San Francisco, where I had planned to introduce my friends to my wife while they finished healing, only to be greeted by an official from the office of Attorney General William H.H. Miller, with a request from the federal government. After consultation with the British Special Supernatural Services Division, it was decided to create an as-yet-unnamed special unit within the Department of Justice to deal with supernatural threats to the United States.

President Harrison and Attorney General Miller, under the recommendation of a one William Tell Blenchy, thought that a certain veteran U.S. Marshal and retired United States Army Officer who had faced those very same supernatural threats was the perfect candidate to head the new division. They had even secured a British agent, one Lady Priscilla Ann Talbot-Blenchy, to assist in the formation of the new unit while on detached duty. I hired William Blenchy as my first deputy and field operative immediately after receiving my commission from the Office of the President of the United States. Then I hired retired Lt. Adam Halfmoon as my liaison to the Indian Affairs office.

"Jefferson, I—" Millie paused and wrung her hands on her apron. "What will I do in Washington?"

I knew I was uprooting her. She'd lived in California for most of her life, moving with her family as child from Kentucky. She'd had to find someone to take over her boarding house for unmarried working women. I knew she was stressed. I walked over and kissed the top of her head. "You'll do whatever you please. If you want, we can find a house to buy and you can go back to doing exactly what you are now. I'm sure there are young, unmarried working women there who need a safe place to live."

"Thank you. I know I'm being a silly goose."

"I'm worried, too, if that makes you feel any better."

She drew back with a laugh and swatted me with her hand. "That's not reassuring at all, Jefferson." She smiled and drew herself up, straight-backed and proud, this woman I had fallen in love with. "Finish packing your trunk. The movers will be here in an hour. I'm going out to find us some lunch since everything I cook with is packed as well." She walked out the door, already radiating the self-assurance I associated with her. I had no worries that she would find her place in Washington.

I turned back to the last of my packing, setting my old saber in a truck next to the unload Tesla rifle and folded cavalry uniform, long faded from its striking blue. I picked up the last piece to pack, a photograph Brinkerhoff had taken, the last photograph before the snake-god changed him. There out of the darkness was the Great Serpent, Snake-Who-Fell in all his terrifying glory, captured by the photographer for eternity.

I wrapped it in paper and placed it in a stiff cloth sleeve. I would hang this on my wall in my new office, with Nicolaas Brinkerhoff's name in gold letters underneath it.

And we would never forget.

ABOUT THE AUTHOR

Michael Merriam is an author, actor, poet, playwright, and professional storyteller. His debut novel, *Last Car to Annwn Station* was named a Top Book in 2011 by *Readings in Lesbian & Bisexual Women's Fiction* and his novella, *Should We Drown in Feathered Sleep*, was long-listed for the Nebula Award. His scripts have been produced for stage and radio and he has appeared on stage in the Minnesota Fringe Festival, Tellebration!, StoryFest Minnesota and over the air on KFAI and Minnesota Public Radio. Michael is a co-founder of the Minnesota Speculative Fiction Writers and a member of the Artists with Disabilities Alliance, the Steampunk Artists and Writers Guild, and Story Arts Minnesota. Visit his homepage at www.michaelmerriam.com

Made in the USA
Middletown, DE
15 February 2022

61280297R00070